THE
BLACK
MUSTANGER

By the Same Author

GONE TO TEXAS

THE KIDNAPPED CIRCUS

RIDE A NORTHBOUND HORSE

THE
BLACK
MUSTANGER
RICHARD WORMSER

ILLUSTRATED BY DON BOLOGNESE

William Morrow and Company   New York

1

The Rikers were two: man and a thirteen-year-old son, hardly an outfit at all. They were just the two male members of a Tennessee family trying to make out by branding mavericks in northwest Texas.

The longhorn in front of them swung around and changed directions with a wrench that would have broken the back of any cattle brute in Tennessee. Dan Riker lifted his reins to pull Sherry around after the dun-colored cowbrute, but the mare had learned a lot in the six months the Rikers had been mavericking. She was around before she felt the shift in weight, and the dun bull had to switch again or be cut off.

On the other side of the maverick, Dan's father was closing in. His rope flashed through the dust, hit the white tips of the long brown horns, and was flicked away as the dun tossed his head.

Dan stayed on the animal's heels. Sherry was too light, the saddle and cinch were too old, and Dan himself was not strong enough to hold the bull if he necked him. The most he could furnish was a heel catch after his dad—if he was lucky—made a successful neck throw.

But the maverick was losing ground. Pinned between the two riders, he was having to turn and dodge each minute, and there wasn't a cow creature alive that could keep that up forever.

Mr. Riker's rope went home, and Dan rode in and made a perfect heel catch. Sherry backed off as Dan took the turns around the horn that Texas called dollies for some reason Dan didn't know, and the bull's near hind hoof came back and back until the maverick's balance was threatened.

Then Mr. Riker sent a sharp quiver down the rope that wrenched the bull's neck, and the dun was down. Dan plunged out of the saddle and ran over to sit on the maverick's head. His father climbed down, too, and started gathering cow chips and sagebrush twigs to make a branding fire.

The big mavericking crews carried a loogan wagon, with bedding for the hands and a water barrel and a fire going all the time in a box of sand, heating branding irons when it wasn't cooking, and sometimes when it was. But the Rikers had to wait for a fire to catch and an iron to get hot, and meanwhile someone had to sit on the catch's head and hold it down.

The fire started, Mr. Riker hog-tied the bull with leather pigging strings from his saddle. Then Dan's work was easier—the maverick couldn't pitch around as much, and he couldn't strike the boy on his head with a foreleg—but not much pleasanter. Ticks crawled and clung to the cow neck, yellow botfly eggs were all down his chest, and flies had come up from nowhere to bite Dan as he waited for the iron to heat.

When the fire was hot enough, Mr. Riker cleaned his cutting knife in it and cut the bull into a steer, lopped his ear in the Riker notch, high on the offside, double cut low on the near. Finally the iron glowed cherry red, and Dan squinched down as hard as he could to steady himself against the shock he always got when the brand bit into a cow's skin. The stink of burning hair and cooking hide came at him, and then his father tossed the iron aside, and they both loosed the hog ties.

As Dan jumped free and the steer started up, Mr. Riker took off his hat and whooped, giving Dan time to get away and to his mare. When the branded brute charged, Sherry had not a bit of trouble keeping herself and her rider away from the sharp, white horn tips. The steer pawed the ground, flipped his ropy tail, and took off in a generally south direction.

Mr. Riker had run for his own pony, called Rayo, before the charge. Now he got down again, kicked the branding fire out, and started plunging the iron into the sandy ground to cool it. Dan climbed down and began collecting the pigging strings.

"One more Prescrip brand on the range," Mr. Riker said. He untied the old Civil War canteen from his cantle, uncorked it, and passed it to Dan, who took a small swallow and passed it back.

"What's that make?" he asked.

His father shrugged and took the tally book from his shirt pocket. Dan saw that the dun made the fifth in a group. Mr. Riker threw a slanting line through four upright ones, then thumbed back. "Two hundred and ninety, even," he said, mopping his dirty face with his reck neckcloth. "If they were all rounded up and handed over, and if the market holds, and if a buyer shows up, that would be a lot of money, allowing ten dollars a brute, minus a dollar to the outfit doing the roundup. Which is enough 'ifs' to water Texas, were they raindrops."

Dan said, "It could all be, Dad."

"Could," his father admitted. "Which would mean

that we could hire us some hands to help us. Four men and a cook, and Prescription would begin to be big on the land."

They branded ℞. R for Riker and a slash through the tail of the R to turn it into the sign a doctor or a druggist put on medicines. They called the brand Prescription, or more often, Prescrip, in Texas range talk.

But they had been mavericking for six months, and no buyer had showed up. The big outfits saddled a dozen and a half men, and they drove to Galveston or Matagorda and sold to the ships that came in there for live cattle, tallow, or hides. They cut out anything that didn't wear their own brand, however. The dollar that Texas law and custom said a man got for selling another's animal wasn't enough if he had to drive a couple of months first.

Mr. Riker looked at the sky. "Another day, another brute, Dan. Let's head the ponies home and see can we shoot us a prairie hen or such on the way. We've eaten so much range beef it's a wonder some cow doesn't take us for her calves."

They rode easy in the saddle, headed for the camp that was still Prescrip's home base. There hadn't been time yet to build a house, nor lumber to build it with in this treeless country, and they couldn't cut sod out of short-grass land.

Six months in Texas, and the Rikers were still

living in and around their wagon. The camp wasn't bad. The wagon cover made a tent, there was a good spring, and granite rocks from one of the outcroppings that ribbed the plains had been built into a fair-to-middling stove.

But they surely weren't living on the high-hog level that the Rikers had heard about back home. Cattle were free for the branding, sure enough, but hard to rope and throw, tie and brand. Furthermore, while folks could eat all the beef they could shoot—and do so within the law—longhorn range beef was stringy and gamey and dry as chewing rawhide.

So when his father started edging Rayo over toward the water hole, Dan looked at the sun and grunted with pleasure. It was about the time of day when wild things came to drink, and there was a good chance of getting a duck or a prairie hen, or maybe an antelope or a deer. As a matter of fact, mud hen would have been worth eating for a change.

The family shotgun had split its stock beyond repair, but Mr. Riker was a good enough shot with a light rifle—which was the kind they had—to knock the head off a flying game bird. The rifle was always with them when they rode, not because of fear from human beings. Who'd rob people with nothing to lose? Who'd pick a fight with a family whose back was against the wall? But an animal sometimes fought hard enough to hurt itself, and Mr. Riker was stern about leaving wounded creatures out on the prairie. He put them out of their misery, even though cartridges were running down to the point where he would take a shot at table meat only twice a week and brood for three days on the rare times when he missed.

Dan dropped back. Rayo was still a little gun shy, but he forgot the gun if he was looking back over his shoulder for Dan's pony, Sherry. The worry about being left alone calmed him down instead of making him spookier. Sherry fought the bit a little, wanting to get to water after a long afternoon of dry work. But Dan held her easily and watched.

Mr. Riker went up to the cattails and arrowweeds that rimmed the water hole at a slow, almost dead walk. His right hand had crossed over already and pulled the rifle from under his left knee. Quietly he checked the load, closing the breech down again without a click. Rayo was looking back at Sherry so that his head was pulled well away from where the gun blast could hurt his ears.

Suddenly Mr. Riker shouted, there was a whirring, and birds went up into the air from the water hole, their dangling feet dripping shining drops back down. An animal darted out of the waterweeds at the same time, but Dan's dad was too old a hand to be distracted by a coyote. The gun blasted; a bird faltered in the sky, and then came plummeting back down with a splash.

Dan had been unable to make out what kind of a bird it was, but he let Sherry go, and the pony shot forward to the water. As the reeds parted, Dan could see the dinner floating on the water hole. A mallard, nice big he duck, light food for three people, but tasty enough.

Rayo was already hock deep in water, nose down and drinking. Dan kicked Sherry over to the bird, scooped it up from the saddle, and rode to his father, who took the reins from him. Then he dropped down into the water, which felt good and cool, and waded ashore. He went a little ways from the mud he'd stirred up, drank, climbed out, and started pulling the feathers off.

By the time his father had watered the horses and ridden up on the sand, Dan had the duck plucked and cleaned, and was stabbing his clasp knife clean in the damp sand.

He tied the duck to Sherry's saddle, and he and his father were ready to go into camp. Mr. Riker patted Rayo's neck as they rode along, saying, "See, boy, good boy, you're not afraid of any old gunshot anymore, are you now, boy?" But Rayo danced a little, still upset by the shot.

Dan knew his father ought to swap horses with him before pot shooting, but Mr. Riker's way was to try and improve his horse each day he used him. He was a stubborn, good horseman.

Supper was all right: duck with salt pork, baking-powder biscuits, black-eyed peas, and dried apple pie for a sweet. Rikers ate plenty; they were far from broke, but becoming ranchers and homeowners seemed a long time away.

After supper Dan worked on his school books while his mother cleaned up. She had been a school-teacher for two years before she married, and she was rough on mistakes in grammar and history, though Dan had caught her, a couple of times, looking up arithmetic answers in the back of the book before she marked his sums. But she sure screeched if he turned away from the problems.

When he finished, they turned the coal-oil lamp out in the tent and sat around the dying cook fire awhile, his dad playing his mouth organ, Dan and his mother singing along. There were books to be read, *Robinson Crusoe* was his favorite, but that was for Sunday daylight. Coal oil—and flour and corn-meal and salt pork and coffee—had to be hauled miles from the nearest store, Stein's at Mirabeau.

The mules that had pulled the Riker wagon from Tennessee were still around, turned out to grass. Mr. Riker grained them every evening, which kept them from straying too far. But still they were big-bellied from filling up on grass, and they took a long time to haul to Stein's and back again. Days that could be spent mavericking were wasted on buying supplies, so the family was frugal with store-bought things.

Dan stripped down and scrubbed himself before climbing under the wagon and into his bedding. As always, he daydreamed before sleep caught him: dreams about a new saddle—black with silver trim— a room of his own with a fireplace, a stove against the winter winds, a root cellar with onions and pota-toes and cabbages, a man to farm for them and fill the root cellar. . . .

*   *   *   *

Breakfast was corncakes with sorghum on them, bacon and coffee. The ponies, Sherry and Rayo, were grained in the tiny corral, made of poles hauled all the way from the Double Mountain country, though graining was not the habit of the maverick plains. Mr. Riker said the usual way was to keep one pony in at night and ride him out to round up the night-grazing horses that were to be used that day. Then he could graze in daylight while the other two worked. But the Rikers didn't have a third horse.

They had cut it pretty fine selling the farm in Tennessee for what it would bring and homesteading in Texas. Still, Mr. Riker had felt the move was the only way to keep Dan and his sons and his grandsons from being the poor farmers Mr. Riker and his father and his grandfather had been.

It was as simple as that, and Dan had no complaints. This life was better than choring around a forty-acre farm and trudging six miles morning and evening to a one-room school.

How it would be in winter was something to make up his mind about when winter came.

That day they branded two cows before noon. Mr. Riker was leaving the cows loose, and next year they would have calves following them. With luck, the calves would be branded Prescrip, too, and the Riker herd would be growing.

They saw nothing for a while after they ate their ham and biscuit dinner, except antelope in the far distance and, twice, stallions on the low granite buttes, which meant that there were bands of mares down below. However, they never went after horses. They certainly could have used an extra mount, but the broomtails and their wild stallions could outrun a cow pony carrying a stock saddle and a rider. The only way to get them was to have a big posse of men, several horses to each rider, and maybe a horsetrap as well.

Once Mr. Riker said, "Dan, we might be smart to hire ourselves out to some of the big mustanging outfits. With a horse buyer on the prairie, they'd be looking for hands. It would be cash money, and that is always good sense to earn."

"Yes, Dad, but—"

"But I didn't come to Texas to be sensible, did you, Dan?"

Laughing, Dan said, "No, Dad. If I wanted to be smart, I'd still be hauling water and feeding chickens."

"Wish our hens had made it through. Sometimes I dream of an egg as big as a house, Son, scrambled up with onions in a skillet big enough for a bed."

"I dream of mine soft-boiled or maybe fried straight up," Dan said.

"I have those dreams, too, but the eggs are bigger in the scrambled-egg dreams."

Then they saw cows again. Dan was the one who sighted them first. He yelped, "Cow critters, Dad," and pointed. Before he could drop his arm, both ponies were off at a full run.

There was a way to run cows, and Rikers had learned it the first week in the maverick country. They hit the band at an angle, and instead of running straight away on those lanky longhorn legs the cows began circling. Then all they had to do was split up, one riding around each side of the cow group. As they came together, the cattle always squeezed out between them, and there always—nearly always—was one left behind that was so anxious to join his family that he could be roped without more than a six-foot throw. Being only a few months out from Tennessee, the Rikers were not long ropers yet.

This time Dan got a he cow, a two-year-old or maybe a long yearling, around the neck with the first try. His father made the heel rope like he'd been born in Texas, and the animal was down. Less than an hour later he was up again and trotting off mad, but bearing the R-slash Prescription brand.

After letting the branded beast loose, they rode for another hour and saw nothing close enough to make a play for. But Mr. Riker was humming as he rode, and when they saw some geese coming out of the sky, he almost sang.

"Dan, if those geese come down to water, I am going to spend me a bullet."

"I never heard of geese in Texas."

"Those are geese, or I am one myself. Strayed off the Gulf of Mexico, I reckon, and there isn't a one of them wouldn't make six dinners. And—hey, Dan, boy—they are circling, circling. . . . They're coming down."

It was a wonderful sight. The geese had been going northwest, near as Dan could tell, in a straight V written on the sky better than Dan could print. Then the leader dropped back, another took his place, and at once the V started curving and circling, coming lower and lower. Finally it broke up, as bird after big bird dropped like a shot out of the sky and plummeted toward the water hole dead ahead of the two riders.

Mr. Riker kept Rayo down to a walk and slowly moved up on the water hole, his rifle out of its boot, his hands and eyes checking the load. Dan hung back, as he had yesterday, trying to keep Rayo's mind off the fact that the rifle was out and about to make the big noise the pony hated so.

Knowing what his son was doing, Mr. Riker let Rayo's bit go loose, and the pony twisted his head clear around to make sure that Sherry was still with him. A final Canada honker came out of the sky, sort of a rearguard to the V, folded his wings, and dropped for the water hole. Mr. Riker fired.

Sure enough, Rayo sat back on his heels a little to show that the gun scared him. But the racket made when those geese came out of the slough, water dripping like diamonds off their feet and their big wings churning the air, seemed like the Battle of Gettysburg.

Rayo, caught off guard, went back some more, and then tried to pitch forward, tangled his legs, and sent himself flying. He landed on the ground on his side, and Mr. Riker's leg was under him.

Dan's heels drummed on Sherry's sides, and the pony shot forward. He leaped off before she stopped, dropped the reins to ground tie the pony, and flung himself down beside his father.

Rayo was half on his back and half on his side, wallowing to get to his feet. Dan snapped the cinch knot loose, and the saddle came off. Rayo rolled and was standing. He remembered to grab the trailing lines; Rayo was too green broke to ground tie.

Mr. Riker's eyes were open. His face was pale, which looked funny on anyone so suntanned, but he managed a grin. "Think I broke my leg, Son."

"Dad!"

"Low down. Below the knee. It'll heal. You better ride into the water hole and get that goose. No use wasting good food."

Dan nodded, unable to speak, and got on Sherry.

He had an idea his father wanted a few minutes to himself while he got used to the pain. Anyway, Mr. Riker was right about the goose; they couldn't waste food.

He still had Rayo's lines in his hand. When he got to the edge of the slough, he tied the pony off to a clump of arrowweed and left him fighting the bit. Rayo was thirsty, sure, but the pony that had broken a Riker leg could wait for his water.

The goose was floating on the water out near the middle. Dan kept Sherry's head high till he was alongside the big bird, then let the pony drink while he hauled the goose aboard.

A gander, and a big one. He must have been twenty pounds or more, and maybe fifteen pounds of meat dressed. But there wasn't much pleasure in him.

Dan watered Rayo while he plucked and pulled enough feathers to clean out the gander's innards; then he left the rest of the plucking till he had taken care of his father. At first he didn't see what could be done.

Mr. Riker told him, "Tear up your undershirt and mine. Go cut four, five of the toughest arrowweeds you can find and bring 'em here. No, do that first, and leave the shirt stripping to me."

He was having trouble sitting up. Dan pushed the saddle behind his father's back for support, pulled off his own shirt, and gave his father his long-sleeved undershirt. He left Rayo tied to Sherry's saddle horn and went back to the slough.

Arrowweeds didn't run to more than two- or maybe three-years' growth before they fell off and gave way to new, green shoots. But he managed to get a dozen second-year growth, and he carried the bundle to where his father lay. There was some color back in Mr. Riker's face.

He had cut the sleeves off both undershirts and left them whole. Now he was cutting the chest into long, spiral strips, working round and round. "Be with you in a minute, Son."

"Sure, Dad. No hurry."

"Got an hour, maybe an hour and a half of sun left." Mr. Riker gulped. "Cut the stitches out of the leg of my left boot there. Be careful you don't slit the leather, and we can stitch her back up again by the time I need to use her." Another grin, more real than the first one. "I'll have plenty of time for leather mending, seems to me."

The big clasp knife, after splitting a goose and cutting arrowweeds, was not too edgy. Dan sharpened it, on the leg of his own boot and then on his broad belt, and bent over his father's ankle. The leg had swollen tight into the boot already. Splitting the stitches, good shoemaker's linen, out of the seam without cutting either skin or leather was close and narrow work.

Mr. Riker, busy with his undershirt splitting, didn't say anything. From time to time Dan had to move the broken leg, and it must have hurt mightily. Still, he never heard a grunt. Finally the leg was split right down to the sole, and the boot came away easy.

"Now," Mr. Riker said, "slip all four sleeves up my legs like stockings. I sure hate asking you to dress me, but then I dressed you many's the time a few years ago."

This time Dan returned the grin, though the joke was not big enough to lift his heart any. He almost threw up every time he had to move the leg and had to hear his father catch his breath.

"Now take the underwear strips, and bind the arrowweeds all around, good and tight. That leg has swelled as much as she's going to."

This operation was no easier. The leg had to be held up in the air with one hand while he wrapped with the other. But it got done.

"Now help me to my feet."

That part was the worst of all. The left leg was stiff from sole to above the knee. Mr. Riker held it straight out before him, grabbed Dan's hands, and finally was standing on one foot. A good half hour had been used up.

Mr. Riker said, "Get the saddle on Rayo while I put this stiff old limb to the ground and see if I can stand on it."

Dan worked with his back to his father. He could hear the breath catching and letting out again. While Dan was still fooling with the cinch knot, his father said, "You're a good doctor, Dan. I can stand on her."

There he was in the lowering sun, pale and clench jawed, but standing straight as he must have when he had been a soldier in Grant's army. "Now," he said, "the problem is, how do we get me on Rayo's back?"

Right then Dan felt good, which seemed impossible a minute before. "We don't, Dad," he said. "You ride Sherry."

"Oh?"

"I've taught her to kneel."

Mr. Riker laughed. His voice kind of grated, but he laughed. "You know I don't hold with foofaraw like that."

"I was just playing with her on Sundays, when there's no work to be done."

"And she should be resting. . . . You're a good boy, Dan. I don't reckon there have been too many things for you to play with, specially since we came to Texas. Well, lead your circus horse over, and let's have it."

Dan brought his pony right up in front of his father, tapped Sherry's knee lightly, and said, "Kneel, pretty please," which was the signal he'd taught.

The pony went down at once, both front legs bending together. Dan untied Rayo from Sherry's saddle horn and led him a good ten feet away. His father's pony was undependable, just a green-broke horse, and might kick out at the worst possible moment.

Mr. Riker said, "Here's how a sack full of sawdust gets on a horse," and turned his back on Sherry. Then he sat down on the saddle, both legs on one side, and said, "Up, girl."

Sherry didn't know that signal, but she felt the lines come up to her bit and stood up, smoothly enough. Mr. Riker swung his good leg over the pony's neck and was astraddle.

Sure enough, Rayo kicked out as Dan was half-way mounted, but Dan was fast and no harm was done. He said, "Where to, Dad?"

"Give them their heads and let's get home."

Dan nodded, used to taking orders from his father, but then he said, "Shouldn't that leg be set? I remember when Lee Bob Manship fell out of a tree back in Tennessee, the teacher sent for Doctor Allen, and he made a big to-do about pulling the leg straight so's it would heal right."

Mr. Riker said, "You and your maw can pull on her if you've a mind to."

"But there'll be men with some of the big cow outfits that would have done it before."

"Could be. But they wouldn't help me. You know a Tennessee Union veteran's got no friends in Texas."

Dan shrugged for he knew no such thing, and they rode out. The Civil War, the War Between the States, the Rebellion, whatever the name, was no real thing to him. His father and mother had not even met before the war started, and they had not married until after it was over. Then Lafe Riker came back to Franklin County to meet the girl whose family had quartered his squad as they rode through western Tennessee on their way to fight the Confeds of eastern Tennessee.

They had married and gone back to his father's hometown, in solid secessionist country, and they had tried to make a living there. Through all of Dan's life, they had been trying.

When Dan first started to school, some of the older kids had called him Bluebelly, but the boys and girls of his own age were as little interested in what happened before they were born as he was, and he had gotten along fine in class.

But his dad had not fared as well. First there had been Reconstruction, which—as Dan understood it—

was a time when Northern soldiers and Northern politicians had ruled the South.

One would think that an ex-Union sergeant would have done well in that period, but Lafe Riker had not been of a mind to use his war-taught skills to help Northerners rob his neighbors. Then the Army had pulled out and left Tennessee to run itself again, and a man couldn't get a loan for seed grain or a keg of nails if he hadn't been something in the Confederate Army.

And so the Rikers had come to Texas, which sounded Western but was really just some more of the South, with drier scenery and larger spaces. The Rikers kept to themselves, and when they went to the store, only Mr. Stein talked to them. The customers were all ex-Rebs, and most of them, to hear them speak, ate Union men before breakfast and had been made generals or colonels for all they had chawed up.

The longer the war was over, the higher feelings seemed to run about it.

3

They came into camp a good hour after full dark. Fifteen minutes away from the slough where he had shot the goose, Mr. Riker had dollied his lines around the horn of Sherry's saddle and bent forward, putting all his weight on his hands.

So Dan had ridden a little ahead, knowing his father wouldn't want to be watched and knowing, too, that the well-trained Sherry would come right along behind him.

He was filled with pride about Sherry. The pony was going to be as good as his father's first cow horse, called Nelson, whom Mr. Riker had ridden and trained for three months. Then he swapped him to Mr. Stein for a month's groceries and the green-broke Rayo, which meant *lightning* in Mexican, Mr. Stein said.

Mexican! Dan hadn't thought of them, and neither, he was sure, had his father. There were Mexicans around, mavericking like the rest of the country or peddling or—a few—raising vegetables to sell to the maverickers. They'd have no feelings about his father's part in that long-ago war, and one of them surely would know about setting legs.

But Dan said nothing on that ride into camp. He would wait and see. His mother might look up, in the quiet way she had, and say, "Lie down. When I was a girl, I was champion leg setter of Franklin County."

So they rode into camp, and Mrs. Riker was quiet enough about the accident. When her husband said he had broken his leg, all she answered was, "Well, hold still and go slack, and Dan and I will haul you off your horse."

"I shot a goose," Mr. Riker said.

"We'll eat it tomorrow, and be glad of it. I plucked greens from the spring, and I've had beef boiling with them all day, with some nutmeg and salt pork to take away the maverick taste. It's a stew that would put heart into a bronze statue of Franklin Pierce." Said president being, for some reason, Mrs. Riker's idea of nothing at all.

Dan got Sherry to kneel again, which caused his mother to cut her eyes sidewise at him. Then the two of them helped Mr. Riker into the tent and down on his pallet, where he lay, white looking and hot looking, breathing hard.

Mrs. Riker said, "Do you need a lantern to tend the horses, Dan?"

"No, ma'am."

"Chunk up the cooking fire as you go by. I'm going to keep putting hot water on your father's leg. We might get it down far enough so we can see how well it's set."

Dan nodded and put a clump of sage root on the fire as he went by. Wood was something they didn't burn in this country. If a person took his wagon to the wooded river valleys, he brought back poles and perches that could be used to hold up a tent or build a corral. But where buffalo or cattle or something had yarded up, the grass gave way to sagebrush, and the roots made pretty good cooking fuel. Otherwise, they used twisted grass, which drove him crazy by burning up too fast.

He stripped the two ponies down and rubbed their backs dry. Then he gave them each a quart or two of grain to keep them tame, standing by to see that the mules did not come out of the night and rob the cow horses. His mother would have grained the mules when they came up; she never forgot a chore.

He slipped Sherry a little extra grain, feeling guilty while he did, because he might never have gotten his father back to camp if the pony hadn't been so doggoned *good* about kneeling, about walking easy all the way in, though it was after working hours and she was hungry. Sherry seemed to know she'd done well. Before she went off in the night to graze and sleep, sleep and graze, she nuzzled Dan's chest. Then she walked off after Rayo.

Moon would be up in a couple of hours, and the horses could start eating.

He put more sage root on the fire under the pot of water and went into the tent. His father, lying on the pallet, looked wild-eyed. His face was very white except for his cheekbones, which were almost cherry red.

Mrs. Riker was changing the bandages she had around her husband's leg, wringing them out of a pan of steaming water. The lines from the corners of her mouth down to her chin had never been there before. When she saw Dan, she tried to smile.

Dan jerked his head toward the tent opening and went outside. His mother joined him by the cook fire.

She said, "He's going out of his head, Dan, for all I can do."

Dan said, "I don't know much about broken legs, Maw, but I think I should have done more than I did. We just wrapped a lot of underwear and sticks around that leg, and Dad got on Sherry and came home. I think I should have set it."

She said, "If your father had thought you could, he would have told you how. I'm not certain he's ever set a leg himself. I know I haven't."

"I wanted to ride out and find one of the big mavericking outfits, where there'd be someone who *does* know how. But Dad said they'd not help a bluecoat from Tennessee."

His mother looked up at the sky. The firelight dug deep into the new lines around her mouth, the old wrinkles around her eyes. "Sometimes it seems a war's never over," she said. "But I think almost any man would help out if it was a case of a broken leg. I don't know, though. I guess it will be your children, or maybe your grandchildren, that forget about that war, Daniel."

Dan took his mother's hand. She didn't pull away, though usually she didn't care for sweet talking or sweet acting. "I've been thinking. Mexicans didn't have any part in the War. They don't care about it one way or another. There are Mexicans around, and some of them might help."

"Yes, they might," she said. "This has been their country for a long time, and it is break-leg country sure enough."

"I'd like to ride out and try and find someone."

Mrs. Riker stooped, picked up a sage root, laid it under the pot where it would catch as soon as possible. "You may have to do that, Dan. I can lay hot cloths on his leg and cool cloths on his head, and then I'm through. Baby colic and the like is just about all the medicine I ever learned." Then her voice quickened and got harder. "But not before sunup."

"No, ma'am. I couldn't go till then anyway. Sherry has worked all day. She would founder if I didn't give her time to put some grass in her belly."

"Stomach," said the one-time schoolteacher. "And you'll founder if you don't get some sleep."

"Yes, ma'am.".

His mother suddenly smiled, the fire lighting up her face, and the smile lighting up the whole night. "You're a good boy," she said. "I won't even tell you to wash up before you get into your blankets."

She touched his cheek and went back toward the tent, carrying the steaming cloths. Dan looked after her, and then took enough hot water out of the kettle to wash up, even if he didn't have to, and crawled to his bed under the wagon. Before he had time to worry about his father he was asleep.

Dawn and the ponies came together. He rolled out, pulled on his boots, and went and got grain out of the rat-proof can in which they kept it. He tied both ponies before he grained them, tied them long so they could reach the ground where their food was laid out. He was going to ride Sherry, but if he didn't tie Rayo, the green-broke would follow him.

Sometime in the night his mother had finished plucking the goose. It was hung from a wagon bow, where coyotes couldn't get it and the night air would keep it cool. Dan found last night's stew and was going to reheat it over the fire when his mother came out of the tent, her hair still down in the braids in which she slept. "You'll need more than leftovers, Dan," she said.

She put a skillet on the fire and sliced bacon into it.

"You get any sleep, Maw?"

"Not to mention, but I'm pretty well slept up. Not much to do around a tent camp while you and your father are out mavericking. I just sort of doze my days away."

"Outside of washing, mending, gardening, and a few other little chores."

"No real work." The bacon was sizzling. She pushed it to one side, and then sliced onions into the hot fat. Suddenly she grinned at her son, jumped up on the wagon bed, spry as a girl, and reached down for the goose liver inside the bird's body. "Give you a real breakfast today."

Dan already had helped himself to coffee. He cradled his hands around the thick mug, drank, and asked the question he had been dreading. "How is he?"

Mrs. Riker dropped the last of the liver into the pan. She wiped the knife blade clean with a rag made from one of Dan's old shirts, and said, "Not good, Dan. The leg swelling won't come down, and it keeps the fever up with it. But he knows me, and he got through the night. That was the worst time. Old Doctor Allen used to say that an hour before dawn was when a fever was worst."

"I'll try and find someone to help."

"There's no one I'd feel safer sending, Dan."

Dan felt his face flushing. His mother usually did not say when she was pleased with him and kept her tongue for when he was wrong.

Dan got up and filled his coffee cup again. "Should I go look at him?"

"He had dropped off into a little sleep last I saw. Best let him make the most of it. I'll warm you some corn bread."

Later he and Sherry rode out, without his seeing his father. He had an idea his mother hadn't wanted to worry him any more than there was a need to. His belly was full, and he had stringy beef and bacon sandwiches wrapped in oilcloth and tied to his cantle. Sherry was lively under him, and the day was still cool and just right for riding.

Dan struck off where he and Dad had seen the dust of riders the day before. There were maverickers all over the land; the big outfits branded and cut and left men to hold the wild animals until there were enough to drive north to the new railroads or south to the shipping ports.

A Mexican outfit would make the same dust as a Rebel one, but he could tell them apart at a distance, because the vaqueros threw much longer ropes than the buckaroos. Almost all of the latter had come out to Texas since the War and were no better with the lasso than the Rikers. They neck caught by riding almost alongside a steer and dropping the loops. But a Mexican cowboy had grown up with a lariat in his right hand, and the vaqueros made a big thing of roping for style and pleasure and sport, not just for business.

So, as he approached an outfit, all he had to do was watch until a man took after a cowbrute, and he knew at once what language his family talked.

Somewhat before noon dust led Dan to a big party of maverickers, maybe thirty men and two wagons.

But they were all short ropers, and he rode a circuit around them. Dan was all alone when he got down and ate his sandwiches at dinner time, and still alone halfway through the afternoon.

He knew then what he had to do. His mother had said as plainly as if she had used words: having gotten through a night, Mr. Riker would live through the day, but another night without his leg being tended to, and he would have few chances.

Dan turned Sherry and rode for the big outfit he had cut around earlier. He hit them at coffee time, which was about halfway between dinner and quitting time. The cook and his helper would have coffee and maybe dried apple pie or prune duff for the men, who would ride in one at a time, eat, drink, roll a single cigarette, and ride out again. It was a nice way to break the hot part of the day.

Dan spotted the cloud of dust that would be the horse herd, held by a kid his age or a stove-up old cowboy, which supplied the riders with fresh horses. Undoubtedly the horse wrangler would keep near the chuck wagon, and that guess was right. As he got nearer, he could see cooking smoke rising thin and blue against the brown dust cloud.

The cook was standing at the tail of the chuck wagon, pounding steak for supper with the butt of a Navy Colt. He looked up when Dan rode in, and said, "Light and rest." He turned and snarled at his helper, a red-eyed old boy without much hair on his head, but plenty on his face, "Give the boy a cup and a slab of pie."

Dan kept Sherry's lines looped over his elbow as he squatted in the shade of the blanket wagon, took the piece of raisin pie and the cup of coffee from the helper, and dipped the pie in the coffee.

Men were sitting around in the shade of their horses, taking their break. One of them hopped down from the blanket wagon—called a loogan for some reason—and said to the cook, "There, that's fixed."

The cook said, "I done sewed that sack up four times, and she always come a-open on me, jest when the night was coldest. Do you stitch her, Will, she will stay stitched. What do I owe you?"

"It's nothing," the man said. "Can't stand to see a good cook sleep with his feet out in the night, even if I don't belong to his camp."

He had a funny way of talking. Dan looked over at him and thought at first he was an Indian. Then he saw that the man might, indeed, have some Indian blood, but mostly he was Negro, like so many back in Tennessee.

Dan got up and rinsed his cup out in the cookie's steaming vat, putting it back on the shelf at the side of the chuck wagon. He said to the cook, "I came to ask a favor."

The cook's face got quiet and closed in on itself. "Well, name it."

"My father broke his leg yesterday. We were mavericking, and his pony came down on him."

"You shoulda spoke up right away. Man with a broke leg who's been laying out all night could be in bad shape."

"I got him to camp," Dan said. "My mother's with him. But his leg's swollen to twice its size, and he's showing fever."

The cook picked up the gun he had been using to pound meat with and pointed it in the air. He pulled the trigger three times, and then laid the gun down again. Most of the ponies held by the resting riders reared back, but even worried as he was Dan was proud that Sherry stood quietly.

"Foreman'll be here in a trice, once he hears that," the cook said.

The dark man who had sewed the cook's sack had been about to mount up. Now he squatted on his heels again, holding his horse's lines. For something to do, Dan studied the horse, a blue dun mare. It was a good horse, but not a cow pony, was his guess. Too big, too heavy in the leg. A good horse to travel on, but slow to turn. The dark man looked like a real horseman, though, the way he sat, his eye never really leaving his mare.

A cloud of dust came into camp fast, not caring if

it scattered itself on the cooking. Then it settled, and a man came out of it, ground tying his horse. "What's up, Doctor?" *Doctor* was what range cooks were called.

"Boy here with a sick paw, Mr. Pasan."

Pasan was huge, taller and wider than Dan and his dad together. The gun at his waist was pearl handled, and the belt that held it up carried a good deal of silver. He said, "You the boy?"

"Yes, sir. I was telling the gentleman here that my dad's pony went back on him yesterday and broke his leg. I got him home, and my mother and I have done what we could, but he seems awfully sick. Neither of us has ever dealt with a broken leg."

"Well, I have. What were you doing when all this happened?"

"Mavericking, sir."

"You're a smooth-spoken one, boy. Eastern?"

"We've been in Texas less than a year."

The foreman pushed his snake-banded hat back on his head and scratched his forehead. Without looking, he held his hand out to the cook. "Coffee. You had a bit of schooling, I'll bet."

Dan felt as if he was walking waist deep in water, but if he lost his temper, his father might lose his life. He said, "My mother was a schoolteacher before she married Dad. She makes me keep up."

"Good, good." Pasan closed his fingers on the cup the cook handed to him. It was a china mug; the rest of them had drunk out of tin.

"Could be I could help you."

"I'd certainly appreciate it, sir."

Pasan gulped half the steaming cup of coffee. "Five minutes one way or t'other won't hurt. I'll want to think what to take out of my doctor kit. What brand you burning, son?"

Dan looked around for a stick. There wasn't one close by, so he took his finger and drew the Prescription brand in the dust.

Pasan drank the rest of his coffee and tossed the cup to the cook, who caught it. The foreman said, "I've seen that brand on cows, and I think me I heard about it. You folks from Tennessee?"

"Yes, sir."

"Name of Riker?"

"Yes, sir. I'm Dan Riker."

The big man made a movement with his hand that said that Dan's first name didn't interest him. "You people fought for the Union, didn't you?"

"I wasn't born till after the War."

"Don't sass me, boy." Pasan shook his head. "No, sir. Was you No'theners I would say you acted natural and according to your lights."

He turned his head and looked over the lounging

cowboys. "You've had a sup and a sip. Now get back to work."

But they sat on, just looking.

Pasan said, "All right, all right, I'm going with the boy. I wouldn't leave a nigger out on this howling prairie with a broken leg."

Dan looked over at the dark cowboy, the rider of the blue roan mare. The black eyes hadn't changed; the thin mouth hadn't twisted. The man called Will must be used to people saying such things.

Pasan said, "Doctor, you got something for me to put in my belly? One of you boys go tell the wrangler to catch me a fresh hoss. You, boy, you can start out now, less'n you want to leave your mare and ride one of my string. I'll catch up with you, your mare being at the tail end of a long day."

"I'll keep to Sherry," Dan said. Sure, she was tired, but she was his. He wasn't going to turn her over to the kind of wrangler this rough-talking foreman would have. As a matter of fact, he wasn't too happy about bringing Pasan back to doctor his father. The foreman was liable to be pretty rough in his treatment.

Still, Dan had no choice, so he mounted and rode out. He had been plain unlucky, running into a Reb and maybe the roughest Reb on the prairie. But he'd seen no others around.

Dan went down a dip in the rolling prairie, and Sherry played with the bit a little at the sight of the green grass in the bottom of the swale. He settled the pony with his heels and started up the other side, when a voice called to him. "Hey, boy."

He pulled up and swung his pony around. The dark-skinned man from the cow camp, the one who had been restitching the cook's bed bag, was calling. "Hold up, boy."

Dan didn't particularly like being called boy, having had a name since he was born, but he held up.

The man came alongside on the blue dun. "What was that all about back there?"

Dan said, "You heard. My father's got a leg broken and badly swollen. He's running a fever, and neither my mother nor I can figure what to do."

In the bright light of midafternoon, the stranger's face was almost blue. The nose was flat, like a black man's, but the lips were thin and firm as an Indian's. Mixed-breed.

"Broke-leg fever can kill a man. Mr. Pasan back there, he was so riled up about helping a Union family that I said I'd set a might of broke legs in my time and would take the chore."

Dan didn't know whether to feel relieved or more worried. Back home, white had stuck to white and black to black, except for a handful of rich folks that had darkies to wait on them. Maybe his father wouldn't let a black man fool with his leg; maybe his mother wouldn't let a black man into her camp. But he'd have to take what chances there were.

The dark man stared at Dan a moment. Then he said, "They call me Mesteño Will. Or Will Mesteño. It's Spanish for mustanger. I'm in the horse-catching business and was just stopping by to deliver some of my stock to Mr. Pasan. What's your name?"

"Dan Riker, Mr. Will."

The mustanger laughed. "Picky about trying the Spanish word, Dan? Mess-tay-nyo."

Dan said it, "Mesteño."

"Now I'm surely no part of being a doctor, but I've brought down the swelling on many a horse leg. A man's cannot be muchly different, even when it's broken, except he has only two."

"We'd be awfully grateful."

"It's not much to do. This is a lonesome country, Dan."

Dan stood in the stirrups, took a look at the sky, figured quickly, and said, "Camp ought to be over there, not more than three hours. I've been riding a big circle since sunup."

"Just ride a loose rein, and your pony will take you home. Horses have more sense than most people."

They settled down to ride then. Will Mesteño

seemed to have used up his talking for the day. He didn't say a word until Sherry started dancing, showing they were within smell of the camp with its grain and Rayo and the mules. Then Will Mesteño said, "I bet back in the real South, the war is almost forgot. I bet it is only the men who couldn't make it at home that goes on telling everyone they meet how they fought for the big, old Confederacy."

Dan was so glad to hear that Will hadn't forgotten how to talk that he laughed.

"That's better, boy. Your dad is going to be all right if a jackleg horse doctor can fix him. Let's let these horses out and make a little time. Ponies can sleep all night."

4

Dan's mother was just lighting the lantern as they rode into camp, greeted by brays from the mules and whickers from Rayo. Dan swung down, and said, "Maw, this is Will Mesteño. How's Dad?"

His mother said, "That is not the way I taught you to introduce people, Dan. Try again."

"This is Mr. Mesteño, my mother, Mrs. Riker."

"How do you do, Mr. Mesteño."

"I'm fine, Mrs. Riker, and I had a mother who was as fussy as you are, ma'am. How is your husband?"

"No change since Dan rode out looking for help

this morning. I surely do thank you for coming, Mr. Mesteño."

"I told Dan, just plain Will does it. The mesteño is a nickname. It means mustang in Spanish—"

"You are Mexican, sir?"

"Partly. My mother was a Mexican Indian lady. I don't promise anything, but I would like to look at Mr. Riker and his leg."

Dan said, "I'll tend your horse, Will. We have grain."

"Blue Streak's not used to it, lad. Don't teach her bad habits." Mesteño Will stepped to Blue Streak's side, and stripped away saddle and bridle with two quick motions. The bridle was a notch-ear, made to come away fast.

The horse went off into the darkening prairie, kicking up her heels at Rayo as she passed, shying away from the mules as though she hadn't seen their like before.

Will looked after them, and said, "They'll make friends soon enough."

Mrs. Riker had taken the lantern down from the wagon tongue. Now she held it high, as though to guide Will toward the tent. The light shone full on his face, and Mrs. Riker took a step back.

Will said, "Yes, ma'am. I'm half Mexican-Apache, but the other half is colored."

Dan held his breath. He felt he had been wrong in not going back and getting Pasan, rough as the mavericker would have been.

Then Mrs. Riker let out her breath, and said, "White, black, or red man, we surely need help from someone, Will."

"Needs must when the devil drives, Mrs. Riker."

Mrs. Riker grunted and walked toward the tent; Will followed her.

Dan didn't go along. He didn't want to see his father lying on a pallet, out of his head and suffering. Instead, he stripped Sherry down and rubbed her back dry carefully. Then he got a split-cane basket and put his pony's evening feed in it. He held the basket in his hands in case Rayo and the mules came back, not to mention Blue Streak. Will might say that his horse didn't eat grain and didn't know grain when she smelled it; still, Dan was going to protect Sherry's supper.

But the pony was not quite finished when Will Mesteño came out. "Dan, you better come and watch all this."

"I have to take care of my pony."

"She is nearly through, and it won't hurt her to miss the last bite or so. I know, I know, it fashes you to see your father sick and raving. But you better watch. If I bring that leg down and save Mr. Riker from being lame or even dead, you will owe the world one man and one leg."

"What?"

"Someday you may have a chance to set a man's leg, save a sick man's life. That will be one debt you won't take to your grave."

While they had been talking, Sherry had gone ahead with her meal. Dan dumped the last few grains on the ground for the pony to snort at and put the basket away in the wagon. If left out, the horses would play with it for the smell of grain it still held, and it soon would be broken.

"Hurry it up, boy. Hurry it up."

The lantern was hung on the post-oak center pole of the tent. It shone clearly on Mr. Riker, laid out on the low cot, rolling around. The straw with which the mattress was stuffed was not rustling; it had been packed down by the sick man's thrashing.

Mr. Riker's eyes were open, bright and staring, but seeing nothing. Dan gulped and felt his stomach drop and wanted to run and run. Will Mesteño's black hand closed on Dan's upper arm and held him still. The dark man said, "Look at that leg, Dan, and don't forget it."

The leg was as big at the ankle as it was where it joined the man's body, a horrible sight. Dan gulped miserably.

"Now," Will said, "we're going to get that limb down to where my fingers can reach the break and feel it. You, Dan. First part is all yours."

Oh, no, Dan thought. I can't.

But the deep voice boomed, "Haul the coldest water you can get from the spring. Usually coldest is right in the middle. Fill two, three buckets. You understand, lad?"

"Yes, sir."

"Go."

As he ran out, almost pushed by the booming voice, he could hear Will say, "Mrs. Riker, I'll thank you for what white cloth you have. Sheets, towels, underwear, anything. If we had ice, none of this would b—"

Grabbing up a pair of buckets, Dan was sprinting for the water hole. He waded in, the sandy bottom firm under his boots, till he was in the center. Will was right; it was coldest there.

His boots squished noisily as he came back up to the camp. Will was kneeling by his saddle, unthonging a pair of pistol wallets from the pommel.

For the first time Dan noticed the peculiarity of that pommel; there was no horn. Many a man back in the South had ridden an old Army saddle, called a McClellan, but everyone in Texas had a horn to rope off.

Will said, "Rest that bucket, and come on in the tent."

Dan followed him meekly enough.

Once in the light the mustanger opened the pistol wallets. But they didn't hold guns; instead, he took out a number of strange things: a lump of tar, a bottle that looked as if it held ordinary fire-blackened lumps of wood, another bottle that maybe held sulphur, and finally a leather package, which he unwrapped. There were strips of bark on it. "Cinchona bark," Mesteño Will said. "Some call it Priest's bark, or Peru wood. Mrs. Riker, if you will kindly put this much"—he held out some strips—"in a cup of boiling water, and leave it to stand until it is cold, I do believe it will aid in taking away your husband's heat. Now, Dan. You see this pile of white cloths? You are to take them out to those buckets you have fetched, and you are to put the cloths in the cold water. When one is drenched clean through, take an end of it, wet as it is, and whirr it around your head, in the air, fast as fast can be. Understand?"

All Dan could say was, "Yes, sir." But he wondered if he had come back with a madman, a tetched-head, as the kids back in Tennessee had called them. Dan looked at his mother.

Mrs. Riker nodded. "Do what he says, Dan."

Dan shrugged and went out of the tent, glad to

leave, but feeling like a fool as he put a pair of long drawers in a pail, took them out, and sent them whirling around his head as he held on by the ankles. The horses must have been hanging around on the edge of the firelight. As the flying drops of water spun into the night, there was the clatter of hoofs running away.

Mrs. Riker passed him on her way to the fire and the kettle of hot water. Dan stopped his idiotic work, and said, "Do I have to go on doing this?"

Mrs. Riker said, "I think that darky knows what he's doing. I have heard of cinchona bark to take away fever, and he had some."

"But waving wet underwear around in the night?"

Mrs. Riker had mixed the bark and hot water in a mug, and she was shifting it from hand to hand as the heat came through the thick china. "I don't know. I only know that anything that helps your father isn't silly."

So Dan whirled. His mother took the cooling brew into the tent, and he was alone again, glad there was no one to see him making a dunce out of himself. A muslin sheet was soaking in the other bucket, the shirt to the drawers in the first one.

After what seemed a long time, Mesteño Will came out of the tent. "That ought to do for this piece," and took the drawers from him. "Start something else going."

"Mind telling me why I'm doing what I'm doing?"

The mustanger said, "Cold. Knocking the water out of cloth makes it colder, for some reason or other. Since heat wouldn't bring the swelling down, cold may do it. I don't know anything else to try, and cold's worked on horse's legs."

So Dan whirled on, through the slowest passing of time he had ever known. His arms ached, and his back seemed about to break. Every little while Will came out and put the cloth he had used in the bucket and took the one Dan had whirled and went into the tent. But he didn't say anything.

And then he came, and said, "You can quit, Dan." His booming voice was high with something that hadn't been in it before. Hope?

Dan asked, "The swelling's down?"

"Coming down. And the night's cold enough now so's I can just hang the cloths up and they'll dry cold. You better get some sleep. I'll want you strong and ready when I do need you."

Dan carried the buckets nearer the tent door and went in. His father's eyes were closed, and his forehead wasn't much whiter than his cheeks. There was a moist and healthy look to his skin.

Mrs. Riker smiled, and said, "The fever's broke, Dan."

"I see. Oh, Will, I—" But there wasn't anything to say.

The dark face looked up, grinning, the teeth looking whiter than any Dan ever had seen. "I told you to sleep now, boy." The dark hand fell on Mr. Riker's broken leg and the shirt that wrapped it. "Bring me a fresh cloth before you go off to your bed." Will held out the shirt.

When it was taken away and Dan could see his father's leg, it did indeed look smaller than it had when Dan and Mesteño Will had ridden into camp.

His mother was paying no attention to him. He went out and pulled his boots off and crawled into his bedroll without washing; he had had all the water he needed for a while.

It was still dark when a hand shook his shoulder, and a voice said, "Boy, the time has come upon us."

Dan sat up so suddenly he cracked his head on the bottom of the wagon bed. "Leg down?"

"Yes. And a man can see where it was misset. If you hadn't gotten help when you did, Dan, your father would be a crippled-up one the rest of his natural life."

Will went away and Dan pulled on his boots, ran his fingers through his matted hair, and stumbled toward the tent. His head felt wide awake, but his body acted as if it wanted to go right back to bed.

The coal-oil lantern had been turned up as high as it would go without smoking. Mr. Riker was wide awake and even managed to smile at Dan. "Son, you certainly picked the right man. Maybe the only right one in all of Texas."

Will chuckled, and said, "You'll not be talking so favorable in a few minutes. I'm about to put a grievous hurt on you. Dan, you and your mother are to get down there at the foot of the cot. I surely wish I had some whiskey to give you, Mr. Riker. Or morphia pills. Or anything. This is going to be an outrageous pain."

There was a leather strap, like a horse hobble, around the ankle of the broken leg. Thongs had been tied to it so that Dan and his mother could both get a hold on it.

Mesteño Will said, "Before we do this thing, I'd like Dan to feel the break, if that is agreeable, Mr. Riker?"

Mr. Riker said, "Sure."

"He may save some other man's leg in the years to come." Will took Dan's fingers and guided them to his father's shin. There was a sharp roughness under the still-hot flesh. "The bone below the break has jumped forward and is trying to creep up. When you are pulling good, I'll push down, like so, and the two pieces should come together."

Dan's mother's whole face was as white as his father's forehead had been in fever. She shut her eyes as she wrapped the rawhide thong around and around her palm, clasped her right hand with her left and got ready to pull.

But Dan kept his eyes wide open as he took up the other handhold.

"Now," Will said. "With all your strength and weight and heart—*pull!*"

Dan flung himself backward, until all his body was leaning against the the thong. Next to him, his mother, her eyes still closed, went back, too. He saw the leg lengthen and Will's black hands come down on the break, and then he thought—but could never be sure—that he heard a click as the two pieces of bone came together.

In a moment Will was saying, "You can let go."

Dan opened his hands with difficulty. He had been pulling harder than he had known. Mrs. Riker opened her eyes, and said, "Oh, thank goodness he fainted," and then would have fallen herself if Dan hadn't caught her.

Will was rewrapping the leg with the arrowweeds and torn undershirts. "Worst is over," he said. "I got a lot of faith in the future of that leg. Dan, you pulled like a mosshorn bull climbing out of a mudhole."

Mr. Riker opened his eyes. "When are you going to set the bone?"

Will chuckled. "It's all over."

"But I never felt a thing."

"That's happened before." The black faced stared up at the lantern where it hung on the post. Mesteño Will took it down and blew the flame out. "No use wasting oil. I stitched up a man's liver one time, he had been gored by a range bull, and he talked to me all the time I was working. It's past understanding."

"Maybe it's the hand of God," Mrs. Riker said.

Day was on them. The east and south walls of the tent were turning gold, and Dan felt tired as he'd never felt in his life before.

Will said, "I'm surely glad that I could be of service to you."

"Great service," Mr. Riker said. "We'll never forget you."

The mustanger shrugged. "Anyone would have done it who could." Which wasn't true. "It's a lone, lonesome country here on the plains, and we got to help each other out."

Dan's mother said, "I'll get us all some breakfast."

"I'll be riding on, Mrs. Riker. Don't bother about me."

"Nonsense. We may be between homes, but nobody leaves this camp with an empty stomach."

The dark man laughed. "All right. You had better feed your husband here light and soft for a while. He's had a bad time."

"I'll do that," Mrs. Riker said absently. Then she

was herself again. "Dan, you go wash yourself with soap and warm water, and comb your hair and brush your clothes. You're a perfect sight!"

Her words made Dan feel better. Things were back to normal.

5

The horses and mules must have been grazing close to the camp. As soon as they heard the people stirring about, they came in for their grain. Blue Streak arrived with them. She had made friends with the Riker animals during the night, but she made no effort to get fed. Dan supposed, as he stood guard over Sherry and Rayo, that a horse who never had tasted oats wouldn't know what they were, but her lack of interest seemed strange. She was acting like a boy who didn't know that sugar was good.

Breakfast was oat porridge and bacon and corn

pones. Will took his plate and went off to the wagon seat, away from the tent, to eat. Dan went after him and climbed up to sit on the near side of the seat. He said, "Nothing as good as porridge with brown sugar and bacon fat in it."

"It'll stay stuck to a man's ribs all day long," Will agreed.

Mrs. Riker came out of the tent, put her hand to her eyes for shade, and called, "Oh, Dan, come here a moment, will you?"

Still carrying his plate, he went to the tent. She said, "Don't you know better than to embarrass that poor Will, after all he's done for us?"

"Mother, I—" He wanted to say he didn't know what she was talking about, but Mrs. Riker was liable to take that as sass, the worst offense she could punish a boy for.

"They don't like to eat with us any more than we like to eat with them," was the explanation she gave. "Black is black and white is white, and they do not eat together."

Dan sat down on the ground just outside the tent and finished his breakfast. But he couldn't let the conversation go at that. He waited till his mother came out and started toward the fire with an armful of dirty clothes. Then he stood up, and said, "Maw. Why did Pa fight on the North side in the War?"

Mrs. Riker came back. "You are old enough to understand, Dan. Your father, and lots more like him in the South, fought for the Union. They were not going to see their country torn apart over slavery, which is against the Bible. To love your country is not to love the colored. Let them go their way and we ours, both in freedom, and that's an end to it."

She went toward the fire again, added water to the clothes boiler, poured in soft soap from an old coal-oil can, and began stirring the clothes, hard, with a paddle Dan had whittled for her when they came through the post-oak country.

Dan finished eating. He got the dishpan and poured hot water from the teakettle in the back of the fireplace into it. Will came up with the pails, and Dan took one and cooled the dishwater down to where his hands could stand it.

Will said, "I'll wash up for you."

"I always do it. It's my chore."

"All right, lad. I'll red up my own plate after. Leave the sudsy water for me."

She was right then. Colored didn't want to mingle with white. He finished, rinsed the dishes with more water from the teakettle, and dried them with a dishtowel made from an old hickory shirt. Will was washing up his lone tin plate.

Dan said, "Will, do you always ride alone?"

"A track-down mustanger has to be alone," Mesteño Will said. "Why, if one of those broomtails saw me with a man, she would never trust me again."

Dan stared, not sure that he wasn't being teased. But Will didn't seem like the sort of grownup who said fool things to kids just to rile them. "How does a track-down mustanger work, Will?"

"Some one way, some another," the dark man said. "My way is, I become a mustang myself. After a while the horses elect me chief of the band, just like Texans electing a governor, and then I lead them into my corral."

"You're teasing me."

"No, sir. I must admit, I'm the only mustanger who does it that way. Others now, they will chase a band and keep it from eating or drinking till the poor horse creatures get so weak a man can rope and hobble a dozen of them out of a single band. But I cannot stand to be cruel. I saw too much of all that when I was back East during the War."

"How was that?"

"I have to be riding," Will said. "I'll make my manners to your folks, and be on my way. I have work to do."

He walked off, a little stiffly, as if he was not as young as Dan had first thought him. But, after all, he had had a night with no sleep at all. He walked away toward the tent.

Dan put the plates and cups in the rack that had come all the way from home.

When Will came out of the tent, carrying his pistol-wallet saddlebags, he whistled and walked to his saddle. Blue Streak came into camp and went right up to him. Then Will did something Dan never had seen before. He heaved his saddle up on his horse's back, reached down, and cinched it before he even reached for the bridle.

Dan, and his father, and everyone else dressed a horse just the opposite. They put a bridle—or a halter sometimes, if one was handy—on the head first, and then held the horse still with it while the saddle went on. Otherwise, surely, the horse would move out when he felt the saddle, and it never would get cinched. But Blue Streak stood perfectly still.

Will bridled, swung into the saddle, and rode over to Dan at the fire. He bent from the saddle and held out his hand. "Your dad was asleep, but I said good-bye to your mother. Be a good boy, Dan."

"Yes, sir." The hand that squeezed Dan's was hard and leathery as a hide left on a fence since last year.

Will let go, and Blue Streak swung around and went out of camp.

Dan watched, feeling strangely alone, which shouldn't have been; he was in his own camp, with his own family. Then he slowly went over and slid his hand up Sherry's neck, dropped his bridle over the horse's ears, slid the bit in, and fastened the throat latch. He wanted to saddle first—he didn't like the idea of any horse being better trained than Sherry—but he didn't dare. If the pony took off with a saddle and no bridle, they could lose the saddle.

Dan got the saddle and blanket off their rack and walked toward Sherry.

His mother came out of the tent, and said, "Where are you going, Dan?"

"To work, Maw."

Mrs. Riker smiled a little, but her eyes were worried and sad. "To work at what, Son? And where?"

"Out on the prairie. Mavericking. Like always."

His mother shook her head and walked over to him. She put her hand on his cheek, just below his eye, and slowly ran it down to his neck. She said, "You're a good boy, Dan. Go take a ride, work your pony a little. I'll see you for dinner."

He stared at her, the unfastened cinch still in his hand. "But—"

And then he realized what he should have known all along. Without his father to help him, the chances of putting a brand on a maverick were just about nothing at all. There might be old-time plainsmen who could do it, but he was willing to bet that even they would have to put such a rough hoolihan down the line that one out of three cow brutes would get their neck broken.

Dan had not been brought up to work that way. He dropped the cinch, jerked the saddle off Sherry's back, and put it on the ground. Without looking, he took off the blanket and put it on the saddle, and then left the pony ground tied as he turned to his mother. "I never thought."

"Nothing to take shame from," she said. "You did more than any boy had call to. You probably saved your dad's leg, and maybe his life. That is pretty good thinking for one boy. I can't see how you could have had more in your head."

"It's a pretty dumb head, Maw."

Mrs. Riker laughed. "Far be it from me to argue with its owner. So let us put our two dumb heads together and figure what we're going to do next."

Dan knew that ever since they had left Tennessee, the Riker money had been going down. True, the number of Prescrip brand cows had been going up, and the first time a cattle buyer came through there ought to be steers to sell, not to mention all the cows that would be dropping R calves next spring. Branding those calves could be done by one man, but it was a long time to spring.

"Just how bad off are we, Maw?" he asked.

She shrugged. "If we cut down on coffee and salt pork, just buy flour and salt and the real necessities, we could last four months. By which time, we would be wearing rags."

"And our belt buckles would be chipping our back-bones."

"Yes, that's about right. It isn't good game country."

"And I'm not the shot Dad is. What if we go on living the way we have been?"

"With sugar and pepper and cloth to make new shirts and dried apples and— Well, you've carried enough grocery lists."

"And grain for the ponies."

Mrs. Riker said, "That, too. Two months, maybe three."

Dan sat on his heels, reached for Sherry's reins, ran them through his fingers. The mare shifted uneasily; it was the time of day to be riding out, not standing around talking. But the best horse in the world couldn't know about going broke.

"Dad'll be walking in three weeks," Dan said. "Will said so."

"If he said so, I'm inclined to believe it," Mrs. Riker said. "But walking how? With a stick. And in a while, without a stick. But that isn't riding. And just plain riding isn't roping. And I don't think plain roping is mavericking."

Remembering the beating a wild cow could give the man on the other end of a rope, Dan agreed with her. On the real ranches up toward the Arkansas line, the men roped and threw a cow six or seven times before they considered it broke to pasture. Maverickers seldom roped the same cow twice.

Mrs. Riker said, "If there were any ranches around, I could hire out as a cook, but I don't know of any."

"The mavericking outfits hire boys to wrangle the horses and help the cook and cut wood," Dan said. "I'll get me a wage-earning piece of work. Surely they'll give me a couple of days off every other week to bring you my money and drive for the groceries for you."

His mother thought a moment. She stared off at one of the little buttes that were the only breaks in the landscape and frowned, though the sun wasn't in her eyes. "Sorry kind of life when a boy your age has to become the family breadwinner."

"It's only till Dad's leg heals."

"Yes. And I know your father'd never consent to heading back home as soon as he can travel, where he could get a quiet job: carpenter, store clerk, teller in a bank."

"No, he wouldn't. He'd say he left home with his nose up and his shoulders back, and he's not returning with his tail dragging in the dust."

Mrs. Riker laughed, a real laugh, "I'll fix you food to take along, Dan. Plenty of it. I don't want you taking the first job you get. There's the business of us

being Union and everyone else around being Confederate, but surely they won't hold that against us,
now that we're in bad trouble."

"Oh, surely not," Dan said. But he wasn't too sure.
He had been in Pasan's mavericking camp, and his
mother hadn't. But he didn't say anything.

He put the blanket and saddle back on Sherry, and
mounted. His mother went into the tent and came
out with an oilcloth-wrapped package. "Corn bread,
ham, and a couple of pickles," she said. "And here's
some money. If you ride to Stein's store, buy yourself
a couple of apples. Might bring some home for me
and your dad, if two bits will go that far."

"Sure, Maw." He wanted to lean out of the saddle
and kiss her, but that wasn't the Riker way, as set up
by his mother. He had never seen her kiss his father,
except on birthdays and New Year's.

So Dan rode out with his head high, looking for
dust clouds, as he had yesterday. There were none
within sight, but he could head in the direction of
Pasan's mavericking camp and be sure to cut their
trail in time to reach them before dark. Maverickers
didn't move far, just enough to leave the small range
where yesterday's work had spooked the wild cows.

But he didn't want to work for Pasan. Safest thing
to do was to go to Stein's first. It was the only store
for thirty miles in any direction, and Mr. Stein could

tell him what outfits were camping nearby. Dan knew the road well, having driven the mules there many's the time, and ridden the wagon with his father driving as often. But Sherry could go three times as fast as the team and end up frisky. He put the pony to an easy lope.

It was still short of noon when he stopped in front of the store, watered Sherry, loosed her cinch, and went in. As always there were a couple of cowboys lounging around, taking a day off to eat canned tomatoes and feast their lonely eyes on the customers who came and went. Out on the range a man could get lonely, and an ugly face could look handsome if it was one he hadn't seen before.

Mr. Stein and his oldest son, Ben, were behind the counter, busy as always. When there wasn't trade, they measured nails into pound packages, swept up, straightened the shelves. Mr. Stein said, "Good day."

Ben said, "Hi, Dan."

" 'Lo, Ben, Mr. Stein. I just want some apples."

Mr. Stein pointed to the barrel, but he said that he doubted if Dan would find any apples worth buying. "They've dried out in this weather. But if you've got two bits to spend, paw through them, and take all you want. The rest we can make into cider, with water and sugar."

"Two bits is exactly what I've got." The apple

barrel was about a quarter full of yellow-streaked reds, shrunk and leathery. Some of them looked more like carvings of old men's heads than pippins.

Dan tumbled the apples around, finding a good one now and then, and setting it aside. At any rate, he was going to get a good deal more than the pair of prime apples twenty-five cents usually bought. The nearest fruit tree was several hundred miles away, and apples were the only fruits that could stand the trip.

Mr. Stein said. "How are your folks, Dan?"

"Dad broke his leg day before yesterday."

Ben stopped rearranging cans of paint, his father stopped pushing bolts of cloth into line. The older Stein said, "What, Dan?"

"Pony went back on him when a flock of geese took off under his nose."

"Well, how is he?"

"Bad at first. But I rode out and found a mustanger, Mesteño Will, who set it pretty good."

"Will's good as a doctor, I always say," remarked one of the lounging buckaroos. "Cured me of swamp fever when I first come into the country. Ain't you the boy from the outfit that brands Prescrip?"

"Yes, sir."

The cowboy shoved his hat back on his head. From his looks, he was what that country called a boomer,

a man who rode his own trail and hired out for a
month's wage when he had to buy jeans or a new
hat. "Man and a boy outfit, ain't you?"

"Yes, sir."

Mr. Stein said, "That's too bad, Dan. Here, take
a couple of cans of peaches to comfort your father.
An active man gets restless when he's laid up."

Dan didn't think that two cans of freestones were
much help toward healing a broken leg, but the gift
was well meant. He said, "Thank you, Mr. Stein. I'll
give them to Dad when I see him. Just now I'm riding
out looking for work."

The storekeeper nodded. He put his hands on his
paunch under the store apron and knotted them in
thought. "That's right. You planned on making your
living by mavericking, and a boy alone can hardly
carry that on. . . . I wish I could hire you, but there's
Ben and me, and of a Saturday my wife and the
younger children help out. It's all this store can
support."

"I wasn't asking you for work, Mr. Stein. I was
just in hopes that you might know an outfit needed
a wrangler or a cookie."

Mr. Stein's hand reappeared, and one of them
stroked his bald head. Dan went back to sorting
apples, but he had gotten all the good there was in
that barrel. "Or any other kind of work."

The second rider said, "Jack Pasan's got a old man working night wrangler that sure isn't up to it."

"Jack Pasan wouldn't hire a Union boy," the boomer said.

Mr. Stein said, "That war has been over a long, long time."

The boomer snorted, but the other rider said, "If I was you, boy, I'd jump Pasan about the job anyhow."

They would push the matter of finding a job for Dan back and forth for a day or more. But if any of them had known of a real job, he would have said so almost at once. Dan took his apples—seven of them—to the counter and put down his quarter.

Ben fished under the counter and brought out a cloth sack in which bacon had come. "This will hold them, Dan, and here's a piece of string to tie them to your saddle."

Dan was thanking the other boy, when Mr. Stein said, "Hey, boy, I have it. Pasan may be everything they say he is, but he likes a bargain. Go sell him the right to rebrand all the steers you and your father have cut and branded. It will be enough money to tide you through."

The boomer said, "Why, sho. You can start over again when your paw is upright and riding, and you'll still have your cows."

Dan said, uncertainly, "Do you think he'd deal with me?"

Mr. Stein stroked his chin with one hand, the top of his head with the other. "I suppose not, you not being of age. I'll tell you what, Dan. I'll write out a paper, and you take it to Pasan. If he says it's all right, then you take it to your father and have him sign it. If he wants to. I'm not telling you or him your business, you understand."

"Yes, sir. I'd be grateful."

"You have nice manners, Dan," Mr. Stein said. "Texas needs people like the Riker family. I hope you're able to stay here. . . . This will take me a few minutes. Why don't you and Ben go back in the kitchen and have a cup of cocoa?"

"Thank you," Dan said. The Stein boy grinned and held open the flap in the counter for Dan to pass through.

Behind the shop there were three rooms, a kitchen and on either side of it a sleeping room, with a bed in one for Mr. and Mrs. Stein, and bunks in the other for Ben and his kid brothers.

Ben said, "Mom is out in the garden. I'll make the cocoa." He got an agateware pot down from the cupboard, took a jug of milk out of the cooling cabinet, and lifted a lid off the wood-burning stove to get faster heat. When he peered into the firebox, he didn't seem satisfied. He added a couple of pieces of kindling through the hole. "Hope Mom doesn't catch me. She says kindling blacks her pots. But when she gets to gardening, it's cold lunch for all hands, and wash your own dishes, if any."

"I'll help you scrub any black off the pot."

Ben shrugged. "Mom isn't as fire-eating as she sounds. It's mostly just noise. . . . Too bad about your father, Dan."

"It surely is."

"I was going to ride out your way, see if you wanted to go rabbit hunting, my day off. I got a pretty good .22."

"Maybe I'll be lucky and get a job around here."

Ben shrugged again, his eyes intent on the milk. A little skin was forming on it. He got out a box of cocoa and put some in a second saucepan, added a little of the warm milk, and started working up a paste with the back of an iron spoon, resting the pot on the unopened part of the stove.

"No jobs around here," he said. "If there was, I'd take one. I sure don't aim to rub my belly against a store counter all my life."

"If I see two jobs, I'll get word to you, Ben."

Ben added a little more milk to the chocolate paste and kept on rubbing. "Aw, I'm just talking. Pop needs me in the store. The kids are just kids, and

Mom'll give credit to any shirttail boomer that comes asking. . . . There."

He slowly added the rest of the milk, holding the skin back with the iron spoon. Then he threw the skin into a pail below the sink, saying, "Waste not, want not, but I sure hate milk skin. There, Dan. Drink that and grow some hair on your chest."

Dan drank the hot brew slowly, letting the chocolate roll around in his mouth. He wondered if there'd be enough money left over from his first pay for the Rikers to have a little chocolate in their camp. He doubted it. Cash pay was short on the maverick plains.

When they finished, they washed everything they'd used with hot water drawn from the reservoir built into the back of the stove. Then Ben drained the water through the sink; the Steins really lived high and mighty.

Mr. Stein not only had written the agreement out, he had put it in an envelope. "I had to leave the price of the cattle out, Dan. Pasan wouldn't like it if he thought I was pushing him. But it should be three dollars, and take two if you have to."

"You've sure been a help, Mr. Stein."

"Where'd me and my family be if all the customers moved out of the country?"

Dan said good-bye, and started out the door.

The boomer cowboy said, "Pasan's working down toward the southwest from here, kid. And I'd rather be me than you, going up against him."

"A rough man," the other cowboy said. "Wants a day and a half for every day he pays for."

On which word of cheer and goodwill, Dan started out on the first business trip he ever had made.

Now the heat was rising in the day. Dan kept Sherry at a walk, but the pony could move out better at that gait than most cow horses. He was three miles and a half an hour from Stein's when he saw the cloud of dust that told him an outfit was on the prairie.

Dan changed direction a little and kept Sherry down to the walk. Even if big Pasan stewed around and yessed-and-noed for an hour before putting his name to the paper, Dan could get back to the family camp by sundown or a little after.

But all trips end, and there was Pasan's camp. This

time the cook was mixing biscuit dough instead of pounding steak. His gun was in its holster. He said, "You again, kid?"

"I want to see Mr. Pasan."

"He want to see you? Boy, he's in one bad humor. He bought himself a hoss from that Mesteño Will yesterday, hoss that Will rode out and around so gentle you'd a bought him for your grandmaw to go to meetin' on, and now Pasan's been throwed two times. It shore made him mad to know a blackie was a better rider than him."

The cook's helper smirked at his boss. "That Mesteño ain't a blackie; he's a hoss that wears pants. Swear if you saw him take his boots off, there'd be hoofs instead of toes."

"You talk too much. G'wan and split me some wood." The cook wanted Dan to know that the outfit was a big one that carried river wood along in its wagons, not a manure-burning camp like most of the others.

"Well, you ever see Mesteño Will take his boots off?" the helper asked, and grabbed up an axe and went around the wagon.

"I'll call Pasan," the cook said. "I could show you where he's working, but if he was to be throwed jest when you got there, he wouldn't look too favorable on whatever it is you're putting up to him."

"Thanks," Dan said.

"Help yourself to coffee."

But Dan thought he still could taste the chocolate in his mouth, and he didn't want to wash it away. So he just sat on his heels while the cook pulled out his big pistol and fired at the sky. Someday, Dan thought, a spare bullet was going to come down on that cook's head and teach him there must be another way of calling his boss.

Dan had left his cow pony ground tied a good distance from the cook wagon; range cooks were mighty fussy about people who raised dust near their biscuit dough or their frying pan. To pass the time, he went over and fiddled with Sherry's throat latch and saddle, neither of which needed adjusting. He was getting nervous waiting for Pasan to come in and listen to his offer of the Prescrip steers, and Dan didn't want the cook or his fool helper talking to him just now.

Pasan came in all right, at a gallop; he pulled up a few feet from the chuck wagon and dropped down in a cloud of grit. The cook didn't say anything. Pasan was his boss.

The foreman was yelling for someone to come hold his horse. Dan studied the animal. It was a beautiful buckskin, with the true black line down its back, black mane and tail, solid black hoofs and lower legs. All the rest of the pony was shining yellow-brown, almost a deep gold, even under the heavy sweat Pasan had put on it.

The cook's helper came skittering around the wagon and took the lines. "Walk her out till she's cool," the foreman said. "If she ketches cold, I'll skin you."

Only then did he act as if he'd noticed Dan, though nobody on the range missed anything new. He said, "You're the blue-belly boy was here yesterday, right?"

"Yes, sir."

"How's your dad?"

"He's going to be all right."

"The black mustanger doctor's good. I'd a gone myself if he hadn't happened to be in camp, sticking me for a bunch of loco horses."

New to Texas as he was, Dan already had seen a couple of animals that had lived after eating loco weed. The buckskin wasn't one of them. However, he only said, "Yes, he helped us fine. But it'll be a long time before we can go back to mavericking."

"Sure," Pasan agreed. "Man with a healing leg can't get down off his horse and hold a wild cow."

"And I can't do much by myself," Dan said. "So I'm riding in search of work."

Pasan grunted. "Scarcer than water in this country, work is."

"I know. I was in hope you needed a wrangler, Mr. Pasan."

The foreman scowled at the sky. He yelled to the helper to keep the horse walking, spat tobacco-colored juice on the ground, and dug it in with the heel of his boot. "Got all the hands I want or need. Good Southern stock."

Dan sighed. "All right," he said. "That being so, I wondered, do you want to buy our he stock?"

"Let's see your brand," Pasan said. "If it's a frequent one, I'd be favorable. We'll be driving to tidewater come fall, and we can use all the head we can find."

Dan knew then that there was something awfully wrong. He had drawn the Riker family brand the day before, and Pasan was too good a cowhand to forget a brand in a day, or a week, or a couple of years. But Dan drew the ℞ again.

Pasan went and stood over the drawing in the dust. He put his hands on his hips as he straddled the brand and looked down at it. Then he squatted on his heels and took a closer look.

"Yeah, I've seen that burn. But not often, and not on no prime stock."

Dan caught his breath. "Mr. Pasan, we've been mavericking ever since we got to Texas, months ago. I don't think we missed a day after our first week putting our brand on a steer, maybe two or more. Not to mention cows."

"You calling me a liar, boy?"

"Well—no, sir. Look, here's a paper Mr. Stein at the store drew up for me, selling the right to rebrand all our Prescrip steers. If we can sell our he stock, we can make it till my father's leg heals and stay on the prairie."

Pasan pulled out a soiled bandanna, and wiped his face and neck. "Don't know as we want your kind in Texas."

"Mr. Pasan, if you mean the War—"

"That, and plain dumbness, too. Don't want the neighborhood cluttered and clattered with a bunch of tenderfoots. Looky here."

Scowling, the big foreman squatted and reached for the stick with which Dan had drawn the Riker brand. The point of the stick hung in the air for a moment, and then came down and turned the brand in the dust into *R̄R*.

"You read it Railroad Connected," Pasan said. "Only a tenderfoot would choose him a brand so easy blotted. Not that any brand can't be covered over. It's the law that protects a brand owner."

Dan stared at the ground. The cook and his helper busied themselves around the wagon.

Pasan said, "I'm not a brand blotter. No use getting hung when cattle's all over the place. But the county law says that a man loses his brand if he leaves the county for more than a year. Which you'll have to do, being a shirttail outfit with its only man down and out. And it says, furthermore and to boot, that only a man growed past his twenty-first birthday can register a burn. Means you can't do anything about Railroad Connected, and it seems to me your old man is not riding to any county seats for a piece."

Dan said, "So you—"

"I'll put Railroad Connected in my name when I've the time to. Why not? This is a hard world, sonny boy, and them that hustles gits; them that lies around on a broken leg loses. You there, bring up that wolf bait."

The cook's helper hurried up with the buckskin. Pasan jumped aboard and swung his rowelled spurs hard into the green broke's sides. The buckskin kicked out a couple of times, and then went out of camp at a dead run.

Dan went over to Sherry and pulled up the cinch without thinking, mounted and rode out of camp, not caring which way he was headed. The cook said something about hanging around for a cup of coffee, but Dan didn't answer.

There was no use riding home, nor back to Stein's. No money to be made there. He ate an apple as he rode, saving the food his mother'd given him for supper.

There wasn't a cloud in the sky, except Pasan's cloud of dust, and it got more and more lonesome as he rode the day away.

Dan felt like giving Sherry her head and getting to camp to tell his folks what had happened. But what was the use? He and his mother could prop his father up while Dad shot Pasan, and what would that do for them? His second thought was to go back to Pasan's camp and face the foreman down, but all that Dan would get for his trouble was to be laughed at, never a pleasant experience.

Hot tears pushed up behind his eyes, but he kept them there. Dan knew what he had to do, which was not tell his father. A man who was down and sick already wasn't going to get well any faster for knowing that he had been wiped out for no reason at all. So that the old War, the War that was over and done with before Dan was born, still was hurting them. How could something that far back work in a man till he turned sour as Pasan was? Dan didn't understand, but the Rikers had to live with the fact.

Finally Dan figured out one thing. He couldn't go back to camp until he had good news to take with him, until something overlaid the bad news like $R\!R$ covering $R\!\!\!/$. His mother would get the truth out of him in no time at all, and she was not in the habit of keeping anything from his dad.

He braced up, looked around, saw a small cloud of dust in the distance and headed for it. What was making it was the two boomers who had been loafing in Stein's store.

They were riding horses that looked about ready to be fed to the coyotes, even though a man could get a good horse and some money to boot just for working for one of the mustanging outfits. The one who muttered that his name was Andy had wood showing on the slick-forked bow of his saddle, where the leather had worn away. The one who called himself Joe had a pretty good saddle, but the headstall of his bridle had been mended with baling wire, passed through holes, and hammered flat with a gun butt.

"Haven't found a job yet, huh Bub?" Andy asked.

Dan gave his name and said he hadn't found work, no. Joe said, "Might as well ride with us, Dan. We're on the mosey for jobs, too."

"Pasan would maybe hire you," Dan said. "He turned me down, but the more riders he has, the more mavericks he can brand."

"Uh-uh," Andy said. "Never no more. I done worked for a mavericking outfit. Twelve, fourteen hours a day in the saddle, and then stand night guard. Not for me, boy."

"But the grub's good," Joe said sadly. "Biscuits every meal, and all the sugar a man wants to put in his coffee. But you gotta have your own saddle, and this old thing of mine would pop right to smithereens if I connected up with a full-sized cow."

Up in the sky three huge birds came toward them, fast. When they got almost overhead, Dan could see that one was a huge winged hawk, its underwings marked in a bright pattern of brown and yellow and white. The others were crows, and they were trying to take away something the hawk held in its talons— a mouse or maybe a small bird. It was not big enough for a rabbit.

Andy said, "You better ride with us, Dan. We're on our way to Galveston. They're building a railroad there, the pay'll be good, and you can always duck in the shade a little when the straw boss isn't looking."

"The trick is to get on the track-laying gang, carrying iron," Joe said. "Eight, ten men on one length of rail, and if you work it right, the other dudes got all the weight on them."

One of the crows charged the hawk hard, its black wings flapping. The hawk let go of its dinner and it fell to the earth, too far away for Dan to know what it was or had been. The other crow dived after it, while the first one drove the hawk away. Dan wondered if being a crow was like being a mavericker. You had to be half of a team to make a living.

"The thing is, Dan," Joe said, "pick a green foreman and get on a crew that is all taller than you. That way they carry the iron up in the air, and you just rest your hand on it and walked along."

"I got pretty long legs my ownself," Andy said, "but it's a good trick for those that are built right. Got any food with you, Dan?"

"Just about enough for supper and breakfast," Dan said. The crows and the hawk were going off in the distance, the hawk heading due south, the crows toward the setting sun.

"Well, we'll divvy up what you got for supper, and hope we spot up a mavericking or mustanging crew before too much of the morning's gone. They'll always feed once, before they find out you don't want to work for them."

"I tell 'em my old maw is dying down in San An-

94

tone, and I don't got time to stop over and work," Joe said.

They were opening up a whole new world to Dan. Back home the dumbest kid in school knew that you had to work if you wanted to live, and the Rikers had brought all their back-home ideas with them.

"Sure wish another war would start," Andy said, shifting in the saddle and stretching his legs. "Those were the days."

Dan didn't want to talk about the War, so he tried to shove the talk off in another direction. "Galveston is too far for me," he said. "I want to be able to get whatever pay I make back to my folks."

"Man, those war times," Andy went on, not listening. "I jumped bounty twice in Indiana, once in Ioway, and twice again in Missoura, once on each side."

"How come?" Dan asked.

"Why, rich man didn't want to go in the Army. He just paid a substitoot to go in his place. I'd take a week, or a leetle more, of training, eating good all the time, and light out one night when the moon was dark and the sentries sleepy. Do it over again a hundred miles away, and draw another bounty."

"You had to be sure and throw your Army duds away, though," Joe said. "I had a better one. All through Maryland and into Virginia, there was rich fellas wanted to be cunnels, so they raised their own rigimints with their own money. They would pay you and equip you to jine up. You could always sell the rifle to some peddler down the road after you left."

They rode along, and Dan was glad for the company. He hadn't known he was lonely till the lonesomeness ended, but he missed his father, who always could find something to look at and talk about, or else stayed quiet. These coffee coolers did neither. Their eyes weren't on the world around them, but on things they had done: jobs with hard bosses, camps with poor food, employers who'd fired them without reason.

Dusk got pretty full, and Dan found a water hole. In spite of the fact that he was a boy, and they were both older than his father, they seemed to have expected him to take charge of the party. He got down, stripped Sherry, and washed her back with the stale water in his canteen. She rolled herself dry and went down to drink out of the water hole.

Andy and Joe slipped their worn, dry-leather gear off their ponies and turned them out, hobbled. Andy hobbled fore and aft; Joe hobbled by the two front feet. The bony horses hopped clumsily down to the water hole, neither of their owners looking after them. A hobbled horse could fall and drown, but a boomer's horse evidently learned to take care of itself.

Dan took his blankets off his saddle and made

himself a bed, throwing a few small stones away. Then he sighed, and took out the corn bread and ham and pickles his mother had given him. Four bleary eyes watched him. He said, "What would you fellows have done if I hadn't come along?"

"There's always someone around," Joe said.

Dan split his grub with them. It would have done for supper and breakfast and a little over to tide him till he could find a cook with a few odd chores he wanted done, but he couldn't have swallowed it under those starving gazes.

Andy did have a coffeepot and some coffee. Sighing at the hardness of his life, Joe toted the water for his share. Dan drank his coffee and rolled up in his blankets. He had had all he needed of the sort of talk his companions would make around their little fire.

Breakfast of sugarless coffee wasn't what he was used to, but he did find three apples worth chewing on in his saddlebag. He laid the rest of the nubbins out for Sherry when she came in and grained her lightly. On grass alone she could have walked both the other ponies into the ground and taken on two more the next day.

While she ate, he stood by to drive off any thief, two- or four-legged who wanted her breakfast. But the boomer nags showed no interest. Plainly they'd never tasted grain in their lives.

Joe was not as easy to handle, however. He said, "That there barley would boil up to a tasty mush, if mebbe we had some sugar or 'lasses or the like."

Dan shook his head.

"Fool kid," Andy said. "Feedin' a hoss whilst good men go hungry."

"All kids is fools," Joe said.

It was going to be a long day.

The dust clouds they saw that morning were all pretty far away, and mostly moving away from them. Dan could have ridden them down and asked for work, but he didn't want to show up with such scurvy company to lessen his chance of being hired. He was pretty sure the drifters would drift now that he had no more food to divvy with them.

But an hour before noon they came on a camp.

"Mustanger," Joe said, saying the first thing that made sense all morning.

"Could be that nigra that they call Mesteño Will," Andy said.

The camp was no better, maybe not as good as that of the Rikers. True, there was a board roof over the one-pallet sleeping quarters instead of just a tent. But the roof was an old wagon bed, its broken axles still in place, and the sides were cattail stalks carefully woven together to make tight, waterproof mats.

Andy said, "They say Will goes off for sometimes

weeks in a row. We better look in his shack for a grub box."

Joe said, "Naw, he wouldn't leave them mares fenced away from water." His split-nailed thumb pointed at a corral, inside of which a half dozen broomtail mares stood, watching the visitors curiously.

A lot of time and work and bought wire had gone into that corral. Like most spots in that country, this camp was one where the horses had better housing than the people. The posts were a foot through, the rails half that, and everything was notched together nicely. The joints were tied round and round with wire until the biggest bull in the world wouldn't have been able to break out.

Andy was muttering that no one, not even a darky, would begrudge a hungry man some bacon and corn-meal. Joe was saying a man could get into trouble stealing from anyone in this Texas country, and all the time he was speaking he was eyeing Dan side-ways.

Dan was sure that if he hadn't been there, or if he rode out now, the boomers would strip the camp of anything useful. He unsaddled, and said, "Think I'll stay around till whoever lives here gets back. Maybe he'll need a chore boy, and I got to find work."

"Work for a nigra?" Joe asked. He and Andy began to laugh.

Dan flushed and said, "Sure glad I'm showing you fellows such a good time. But nothing here says it has to be Mesteño Will's camp. Could be a mavericker, who's just got some mares up for breaking."

"Could be," Joe admitted. "Well, let's wait around, and maybe he'll be in for dinner, whoever he is. Then I gotta be moseying on."

"Me, too," his partner said.

After less than a day with them, Dan was sure that nobody and nothing anyplace in the world was waiting for either of the boomers except death.

To kill time without having to listen to the aimless chatter, Dan walked over to the corral. Sherry, with hardly any work since her moonlight grazing, went after him, nickering a greeting to the penned-up broomtails, which they returned.

The top rail was well over Dan's head, making the mares inside look small. But they weren't much smaller than Sherry, somewhere between thirteen and a little over fourteen hands each. Broken, they would make good cow ponies. There were no swollen hocks or hammerheads among them.

Mesteño Will rode in during midafternoon. He didn't seem surprised to see the boomers lounging in his dooryard, but his dark and hard gaze rested full on Dan's face for so long that Dan fidgeted.

Will said, "What you doin' here, lad?"

Andy said, "He's riding with us. We're looking for work. Got anything to eat, Uncle?"

"I'm not your uncle, and give me a reason or two why I should feed the likes of you."

Both Joe and Andy got to their feet at once. Dan had not known they could move that fast. Joe said,

"Watch your black tongue when you talk to a white man!"

"Gun doesn't care what color finger's on the trigger!" Mesteño Will said.

The boomers folded. "We ain't had a bite since last night." The whine in Andy's voice made Dan sick, but it didn't seem to move Will.

Dan said, "If you have any chores, I'll do them and pay for our grub."

The three men stared at him as though he were a horse that had said: "Excuse me."

Finally Will answered, "There's always chores around a horse farm. You can feed and water the mares in the corral."

Obviously the drifters felt that a white boy shouldn't do chores for a black man. But what they didn't know was that Rikers didn't beg their feed. Dan asked, "Do they get grain, Will?"

"No. Just give them each a double fork of hay. Spread it around good so they all get some without undue fightin' an' squabblin'. You'll have to haul their water in buckets. They ain't broke to lead just yet."

Dan said, "All right."

"Water first, so's they don't wash the good hay out of their belly." Will turned away. "I'll fix some vittles."

The water buckets were made of leather, cavalry style. Dan carried two of them down to the water hole, where Sherry and Will's blue-roan mare were snorting and kicking water.

Dan grinned at Sherry, because she was enjoying herself so, and toted the water up to the corral. The drinking trough was made of planks robbed from some old wagon bed and tarred together. It took three trips before the mares stopped drinking and began whickering for their hay.

The hayfork was just inside the wagon-bed shack, out of the weather. Will was inside the shack, where he was starting a fire in the stove. They didn't say anything to each other. Dan carried the fork down to the fenced-in haystack, the mares following as far as they could inside their corral. They must have been fenced in awhile to learn the meaning of a fork.

He had thrown the first two forks of hay into the corral when Andy came strolling down to the haystack. "Kid, I don't know your folks, but the way old Stein talked to you, they is nice people. They wouldn't want you doing thisaway."

Which was probably true, but nothing in his time with Andy had made him feel like taking advice from a saddle tramp. Dan hooked the fork deep into the hay and swung a heavy load around. Andy had to duck to keep from being hit by the fork handle, and then he had to step aside to keep from being speared.

Two of the mares were eating; the others stood back. The first one would be the boss of the corral, the second her straw boss. As soon as they were thrown together, horses worked out who could boss who. Two more mares started chomping, and Dan went back to the haystack.

Andy was still there. "All I'm telling you is, well, is just what your own daddy would tell you if'n he was here."

Dan remembered what Mesteño Will had said, "You're not my daddy."

"Mebbe so, but I'll bet you he didn't raise you to work for a darky."

Dan forked more hay and carried it to the mares. Sherry came up from the water hole, Will's blue-roan mare with her, and they followed Dan into camp. Then they turned away and went out foraging. The drifters were squatted on their heels, eating beans and fried steaks and biscuits with frying-pan gravy. Dan took his plate and squatted down with his back to the shanty, sawing his meat up with his pocket knife and a tin fork Will had put on the dish. He could have used more salt, but Will had walked away toward the corral and was watching the mares eat.

Andy and Joe had finished their meal. They went and got their horses, which had been standing around ground tied. The saddle tramps pulled their cinches tight. "Finish your grub and let's go, Dan."

Dan looked from Andy to Joe, and said, "Hey, you left your dishes on the ground."

"The nigra can pick them up."

Dan made up his mind. Keeping his voice friendly, he said, "This is as far as I go, fellows. When I finish supper I'm riding back to my folks' camp."

The drifters looked at each other and shrugged. Will turned from watching the mares, which were now using the watering trough, and leaned back against the high corral rails, watching his guests. The boomers rode out without saying good-bye to him.

Dan finished eating, went over and picked up the other two plates, took all three into the shack, and got hot water from a big tea kettle on the back of the stove.

Will came to the door, and said, "No call to do that."

"Way I was brought up."

"To be sure."

The sky was filling with birds finding a good spot to pass the dark hours. Dan took the washed plates and forks to the shack, and Will took them from him. Dan said, "I'd better be getting on."

"Be too dark to find your way pretty soon."

"Still—"

"Camp here tonight if you've a mind to. How come you didn't ride on with your friends?"

"No friends of mine," Dan said. "Why, it seems nobody'd hire anyone who's riding with them."

Will shoved his battered hat back on his head and grinned slightly. "I see what you mean. Well, camp here, and I'll give you breakfast. A man wearies of scrubbing up after his own cooking."

"Thanks, Will."

"To be sure."

Dan spread his bedroll out down toward the corral. Sherry came in, and he grained her. After a while he went down to the water hole and stripped down and washed himself.

When he came back, Will was in the cabin eating by the light of a candle. Dan wasn't tired, but he stretched out on his blankets, his head on his saddle, and watched the stars come out, one by one. Some sort of night swift or swallow or whatever was skimming around over the camp. His father had told him that those birds flew with their mouths open and lived on the bugs they caught that way. Never was a bird in the world worried about getting a job.

This thought made him chuckle a little, but the laugh died. He would have liked Sherry to come up and bed near him, but the moon was rising, and she would want to use the light to graze by.

Will came out with his bedroll and stretched it in front of the shack. Dan wanted to move closer, so they could talk a little before they went to sleep, but if white didn't eat with colored, they surely didn't sleep side by side.

After a while he fell asleep.

When Dan woke up, dawn was just yellowing the sky a little. He pulled on his boots and hat and hurried to the corral. Washing a few dishes wasn't enough to pay for his meals, and he wanted to get the mares tended before Will got out of his bedding.

Will had the fire going when he finished. "Bacon, biscuits, sorghum, and steak for breakfast," he said. "I got work to do. . . . Lad, you want to make a few dollars?"

"Why, sure."

"Got to drive those mares to an outfit that's heading for Missoura. Back in the farm country, they'll pay good money for a mare that's gonna drop a foal come next spring. They grain up the mare all winter, and the colt's born strong and healthy. Then they breed the mare back to a good stud, Steeldust or Morgan maybe, and get a second colt next year. Good business."

"Hey, that sounds all right."

"Well then, fetch us two plates and forks, and we'll strengthen our bodies," Will said.

Dan went to the cabin and found Will had left his own plate unwashed after supper. Dan's mother never would have stood for that, but a man could get careless, living in a camp with no ladies around.

Dan took his dish and ate hungrily, his back to Will. The fresh biscuits tasted just fine; he ate four of them. Then he gathered up the plates and skillets and gave them a good scrubbing over the fire. The coffeepot was nearly empty, so he drained it and washed it out, putting everything back in the shack.

"About that money I held out to you," Will said. "It would come to five dollars and your feed. Take maybe two, three days, no more."

Dan hesitated. He never had heard of a white man or boy, working for a colored. On the other hand, anybody ought to understand. His father's leg was broken, and there weren't any other jobs that he had heard of around.

Will let out a shrill whistle, and then went to get together Blue Streak's gear, confident that she'd come on that one sound. Dan went to get his own saddle and bridle ready, and fooled with his saddle blanket, pretending to scratch a spot off it with his fingernail.

Five dollars for three days' work was more than he had expected. Dollar a day was going pay for man, and a boy couldn't count on much more than half of that, four bits. Five dollars meant that the Rikers could hold out one week more. But—

Blue Streak came into camp, Sherry close behind her. Dan said, "I'll take the job, and thank you kindly."

Will just nodded.

When they were saddled and ready, Will said, "You mount up, and get ready to turn back any silly mare that tries to depart from the bunch. I'll open the corral."

Dan stood in the stirrups, reins high, ready to show Sherry what he wanted done; she never had herded horses. And, in truth, one dun mare did break from the bunch and start across the prairie, but Sherry ran her down and headed her easily, shoving her back to where Will was pushing the band out to the northwest, making little clucking sounds in his throat and sometimes whistling.

He said, "I'll ride point and you ride drag till we are certain sure they are following me, Dan. Small bunch like this, they won't raise more dust than you can eat."

Point was head of the herd, drag the very back, the rearguard, so to speak. Dan wondered how Will would have made out all alone, and when the mustanger waved his arm for Dan to come up and ride alongside him, he asked.

"If I had to, I'd a neck yoked 'em, two by two, like Noah's beasts goin' into the ark. And maybe led that buckskin lady, she's boss of the herd. Neck-yoked, one of them would surely want to stay with the family, and the other would only halfway want to cut up fancy. But if one of 'em busts out Blue Streak can run her down quick an' easy, the broomtails carryin' colts like they do."

Dan twisted in the saddle and looked back at the mares, quietly following along. "How can you tell when a mare's in foal?" All of them had swollen bellies, since they had been feeding on grass instead of grain or good hay.

"By their eyes," Will said. "You'll see, if you're the kind to make a horseman, which you are."

"I'd certainly like to be. But there's just Dad and me, and no money to hire hands or build a big horse trap."

"You know how I catch horses, lad?"

Dan said, "No, but I'd like to hear."

Will nodded. "Some men crease them. You know what that is? They say if you shoot a horse right on the crest of his neck, he will fall down out of his mind and stay that way long enough for you to get pigging strings on him. I dunno. Every fool I've ever seen tried it, either missed or killed the horse. Or worse, wounded him bad and let him get away."

Will moved his mouth, chewing his tongue as a man did to moisten his throat. His eye was on a distant butte, crowned—as few of the buttes were—with some warped trees that looked like junipers. "Then there's the roundup for a big gang of men," Will said. "You make a big corral, in maybe a box canyon, so you only have to build the front. Then you get ten, twelve riders, and they surround three sides of your horse band, and sooner or later they can get it to where it goes into the corral. Most of the men ride in and hold the broomtails at the back of the corral, while the rest close the gate."

"You ever do that?" Dan asked.

"Yes, and it's fun. It's the wildest riding you'll ever get. But a long time back I decided to go it alone."

Will stopped talking and looked off at the butte again. In some hidden coulee, some sort of birds—ducks, or maybe just coots—were talking to each other. If they had a gun, they could have gotten fresh fowl to eat, but Dan had left the family gun in the family camp, and he'd seen no sign of any hunting weapon in Will's camp.

"I been alone a long time," Will said. "Just me and the horses. And you know something? Out with the horses, you can wait and wait, and not one of them will say anything you haven't heard before."

Dan looked at him. Not a muscle of the mustanger's face moved, but his eyes seemed brighter than usual. Dan took a chance and laughed, and slowly the dark features relaxed in a smile.

"So," Will said, "creasing is just plain no good, and rounding up is for a big outfit. There is left walking down. I've never heard of any but those three ways of getting yourself a wild horse, moreover a bunch of them."

He paused again, and then went on. "Now walking down takes two men, better three. You keep the band moving, one man riding after them, the other two resting their horses and maybe graining them, and all taking turn and turn about. If one man was to try it, his horse would play out under him long before he could get a rope on any in the wild band. Broomtails are fast on their feet and used to going without graze. So what does it all add up to?"

Dan felt himself frowning as he turned over everything Will had said. "Why, it sounds like one man alone can't catch a wild horse," he said finally.

Will's laugh was loud and clear and happy. "That is right," he said. "That is *exactly* right. But there is Blue Streak to show I *can* catch a horse, and there is that bunch of mares to show I can catch a whole bunch of horses. Why, half the mavericking outfits around here have bought horses from me."

"But—"

"Yes, but," Will said. "Well, Dan, I'm not going to tell you. Maybe someday you'll have a chance to see for yourself."

But Dan didn't see how, since Will always worked alone, and no other man seemed to use his way of mustanging.

And then Dan realized that he wanted to work for this black man for good, and not just for a day or so. That was a wrong way to think, as any cowboy, mavericker, or saddle bum could tell you. But it was the way Dan was thinking, and there wasn't much he could do about that.

10

Driving the mares to where they were to be sold—
the buyer was a horse dealer named O'Donnell—
wasn't really work. Will led the way, and the mares
followed along nicely enough, with Dan once in a
while riding back to the drag and all around the herd,
pushing back stragglers.

They camped early the first night, near a butte from
which a spring trickled. While Dan stayed below and
watched the mares drink, Will climbed to the top
and looked all around.

When he came down, he said, "All right, so far as

I can tell. Just before dark I want you to skin up there and make sure no wild bands are nighting it nearby. These mares are good enough old gals, but does a wild stallion come whistling at them, they just might take off with him."

"Okay," Dan said. "There's brush up on the butte walls. I'll fetch up some dead wood for cooking."

"That's what I git for hirin' a boy 'stead of a man," the dark mustanger said. "Always thinkin' about his next meal."

This time the dead face and the bright eyes were signs Dan knew. He laughed, and Will smiled back at him.

They ate before full dark was on them, and ate pretty well, too. Will had a little screw-top pot tied to his saddle, in which red beans and mesquite pods had been soaking all day. The mesquite flavored the beans, Will added chili and the grease from their bacon, and the mess was as good as a man—or boy—could ask for.

After he had washed up, Dan climbed the butte, enjoying the breeze that dusk was bringing. He walked all around the small tabletop and looked out carefully, but there were no horses in sight; just one old mossy-horned loner of a cow, gloomily settling down for the night.

"Still and all," Will said, when Dan reported,

"we'll take turn and turnabout through the night. We got the mares this far, be a shame to lose them."

He took the first hitch, Dan the second, and then, sometime after midnight, Will woke him again. "Watch till you're sleepy, and then give me a nudge," he said.

But Dan, sitting by the fire, and once in a while standing up to make sure the mares were not restive, found he didn't need any more sleep. The day had been easy, and he liked to sit up and look at the stars and hear a coyote here and there yelping how hard it was to be born a coyote.

From all his maverick chasing, Dan had become a fairly good prairie man. He looked at the North Star and then, as daylight grew, at the buttes in the distance and he lined out where his home camp was. If they didn't go any farther today than they had yesterday, he could be home in a good day's workout for Sherry, home with the first cash he ever had made and ready to figure out where he'd make the next piece.

That day's ride wasn't even as long as the first one's. They were into O'Donnell's camp by midafternoon, coming in with a rush, the mares smelling the water hole by which the horse dealer had camped.

O'Donnell's riders came in, one by one, from grass herding his string of horses and looked over the mares. They looked over Dan and Will, too. Most of them said hello to Will, but not a one of them spoke to Dan.

Will and O'Donnell dickered in low voices, and finally money changed hands. Will went to the chuck wagon to get coffee, and O'Donnell was alone.

Dan went up, and said, "Mr. O'Donnell."

O'Donnell looked at him the same cold way the cowboys had, and said, "Yes?"

"I'm looking for work," Dan said.

"Seems to me you got you a job." The accent was Southern, but different from either Texas or Tennessee. Missouri, maybe.

"Job just ran out," Dan said. "Will hired me to help drive here."

"Will? Ought to call your boss Mister Will, boy."

Dan said, "He's a nice man to work for."

O'Donnell looked at the sky. "That could be," he said slowly. "But it is agin nature for white to work for colored."

Before he thought, Dan asked, "Why?" and then at once was sorry. There went his chances of working for this outfit, he was sure.

But O'Donnell didn't flare. He took his time, and said, "Durned if I know, that's the way it is. And it don't pay to go against nature and custom, that you'll find as you age up a bit. Coming to which, you a runaway?"

"No, sir. My dad and maw are camped about a day's ride up that way. Paw and I were mavericking until he broke his leg."

O'Donnell nodded. "I was wondering," he said. "Well, when Will pays you off, you take that money back to your folks, and next time you better ask them before you hire out to just anybody. Not that Will isn't a good man. He's the best mustanger I know, and what he tells you about a horse, that is the truth and all the truth."

"Yes, sir. He surely knows horses."

"Half horse himself, or maybe three quarters. But that don't change things."

"How about that job, Mr. O'Donnell?"

"Wouldn't do. My boys wouldn't work alongside you after seeing who your last boss was."

"All right, sir."

O'Donnell opened his mouth as though to say something more, and then closed it again.

Dan slowly walked over to Will, who said nothing, but took out the roll of greenbacks that O'Donnell had given him, peeled off a five, and handed it to Dan.

Dan said, "Thanks, Will."

"You earned it, Dan."

That was that. Nothing left to do but climb aboard Sherry and head for home. But Dan stood there until Will finished his coffee and cinched Blue Streak up and rode out. Then Dan got into the saddle and loped after him.

Over the first roll from the camp, out of the sight of the horse drovers, Will said, "You're paid off, Dan. Ride for home and brighten your good mama's heart with the sight of money."

"No hurry. Thought maybe if I rode with you, I'd learn something about mustanging."

Will just snorted, and Blue Streak and Sherry tensed up, ready for orders. When they didn't come, they dropped back to a shuffle again.

They went on that way for perhaps a hundred yards, and then Will said, "I dunno, just don't know. . . . Look, lad, that five dollars you got. Ride it home to your folks, and see what they say. Even was you colored, I'd not take you out mustanging without your folks' say-so, you bein' young as you is."

"Where'll you be, Will?"

"At the camp, where else? Be good to sleep in a coupla mornings, with no mares to tend to."

"All right, Will."

"You're not there in second dawning, I'll know they said no."

Dan nodded, looked around at the buttes, chose his line for home, and started Sherry out.

11

It was close to dark when Dan felt Sherry quicken and heard Rayo whickering a greeting. As he neared camp, he passed the wagon mules, cropping uphill from the water hole. They looked up, one of them brayed, and then they went back to eating.

His father was out of the tent, propped up against a wagon wheel. He called, "Man, I thought you had gotten yourself a wife and left us, Dan."

Dan swung down from the saddle and found it hard not to run over and kiss his father, as he would have done a couple of years before. There was some color back in Mr. Riker's face, and the thick willow stick next to him showed he was beginning to get around a little by himself.

Dan's mother came out of the tent, and said, "So you're back," which was so much like her that Dan laughed till even his mother smiled a little. His father was laughing as hard as Dan was.

"I've got a job," Dan said, and took the five-dollar bill out of his pocket and handed it to his mother.

Mrs. Riker turned it over, seeming to read both sides of it. "Well," she said to her husband, "take your time about getting well. And I am going to hire myself a hired girl. It wouldn't be suitable for a millionaire's parents to work."

Mr. Riker said, "Five dollars, and you've been gone less than a week. If there were railways in Texas, I'd think you had been holding up a train."

It was good to be back being teased by his father, but even better to hear his mother making one of her rare jokes.

Quickly as he could, he told them all that had happened to him. Mr. Riker stopped smiling when he heard how Pasan was going to blot the R brand into RR connected. He said, "He wouldn't do that unless he thought we Rikers were down and out." And no more was said about the loss of those months of work. Mr. Riker believed, and had taught Dan to believe, that it didn't pay to fret over something you couldn't do anything about.

Dan went on with his story.

When he finished, Mr. Riker raised his hands off his lap a little, let them fall back again, and looked at his wife. "It's up to you," he said.

Mrs. Riker was not one to hurry. She went into the tent saying, "You'll want to eat. We've supped."

Dan sat down on the ground next to his father. "Leg hurt much?"

"Not to notice." That reply seemed to put a stop to any more talk. Mr. Riker's mouth was shut tight, just the thin slit it got to be when he had asked his wife to make a decision and was waiting for her answer.

Mrs. Riker came out of the tent and handed Dan a bowl and a fork. "Rabbit stew," she said. "The Stein boy came by and gave me a brace of fine cottontails. His folks sent me some tea, too. Good people."

Dan forked the stew down and drank the gravy out of the bowl. His mother never would have allowed that a week ago, and she had forgotten to tell him to wash up before eating, too.

They waited on her answer, and Dan wasn't sure what he wanted it to be. Mustanging sounded like the best job in the world, but being looked down on by all the whites in Texas didn't seem very favorable.

Finally his mother said, "I never thought my boy'd

be working for a darky. But then I never thought I'd be living in a tent either."

Mr. Riker sighed. "Nor nursing a broken-legged husband a couple of dozen miles from nowhere at all."

Dan said, "Then it's all right?"

"Mustanging," his mother said, "roping wild horses. Two men alone. . . ."

"Will's been doing it a long time, and he's not stove up."

"Crippled. Or injured. Or even just plain hurt."

"Yes, ma'am."

"But you don't start back till you've had a good night's sleep. And a bath."

And that was all the Rikers ever said about a Tennessean working for a black man.

12

As he neared Will's camp, next night, the light was still good. But when he rode into the camp itself, Mesteño Will was not in sight. Dan unsaddled, rubbed Sherry down, and turned her out before Will came out of the shack, rubbing his eyes. "I've been taking a nap out of the sun," he said.

"Well, take it easy. Any chores need doing?"

"Aw, take it easy your own self." There was a long pause. Will looked all around the sky, as though worrying about rain. "You here to stay?"

"Why not? It's a job, isn't it? Mother sent you a fried apple pie."

He could see Will's face unstiffen. "There haven't been too many pies in my life," the mustanger said. "You ever eat roasted mescal root?"

Dan shook his head.

"You will before you're through. Mebbe I shoulda told you to stay home till you learned to make pies like this."

The next day they rode out with sunrise streaking the sky.

"Should be some nice mescal right over there," Will said, looking around. "Right at the foot of that butte." He turned Blue Streak and started off toward the butte, although it was miles away. Dan wondered what mescal had to do with mustanging.

Will rode with his chin down, pointing at the near side of his horse. Once having headed Blue Streak, he seemed to count on the pony's knowing which way to go and why. Will also seemed sure that the roan wouldn't put her foot in any gopher or ground-squirrel holes.

Not so sure, Dan rode with his eyes all around him, on the butte, on the ground ahead, on either side. Twice he saw mavericks and almost lifted his lines to run them down before he remembered that, since his father's accident, he was no longer a cow chaser.

Too bad. If he had brought the ℞ iron, maybe he could have asked Will's help in branding a cow or two. Then Dan remembered that the Riker brand could be blotted, and that putting it on new cows was just helping Pasan and his stealing riders.

So he settled down to ride. It was a nice day, maybe a little too warm, but then summer was growing. There was just enough breeze to dry a man's hair when he took his hat off, but not enough to raise dust; just enough clouds to throw a cooling shadow now and then, but not enough to cause a worry about sleeping out in the rain.

By now Dan realized they would not get back to camp before dark. The butte they were riding for was more than a half day away.

The mescal that Will had been seeking turned out to be what the Rikers called agaves. When Dan told Will, he smiled. "They got as many names as any family pet. I have heard them named pitas and lechugillas, and my father said that back where he came from they was called century plants. Given enough of them, a Mexican can just about make out to live. You can dry the leaves and make rope, collect the sap and make beer. They will grow into a fence do you want them to, and the roots make soap. But I'm going to show you how they make the best kind of food for a man who is mustanging. Now. Take your saddle axe and go up on the butte and drag me down a lot of dead greasewood."

As they were riding up, the butte had seemed to rise straight up off the prairie. Now that they were right under it, however, Dan could see that there were all sorts of paths, weathered into the cliff, up which a boy, or a man or even a good pony, could climb. He chose to walk. Will had Blue Streak so hardened that the roan pony seemed able to go days without eating. Sherry, who was used to grain she no longer got, needed every minute of grazing she could manage.

There was pretty good grass, with greening seeds, among the mescals. He slipped Sherry's gear off and turned her out to graze, while he took the saddle axe from behind the cantle and began to climb the rubbly butte.

Sometime it had rained a lot around here, and the shrubs had grown thick. Then normal weather had come back, and half of them had died. He hardly needed the little axe; sun and wind had dried the stalks out till they broke when he kicked them. But thorns were thick. He cut and chopped, and finally wrapped his belt around a bundle to save his hands.

Down on the level, Will was busy cutting the stalks out of the mescals. Only about one in eight of them had shot up and left a stalk towering high above the spiny leaves. Of these, only about one in three was still green and fresh looking.

They were the ones Will selected. Having picked

them, he cut off the top foot and a half of the stalk and threw the rest away. "We need about thirty," he said. "And about ten bunches of wood like the one you've got."

So they wouldn't finish that night. There was about another hour of light left, and Will had three mescals ready for roasting.

Dan went back up on the butte and cut wood as fast as he could. Really, it wasn't wood, just twigs, but it had seemed to satisfy Will.

This time Dan took the rope off his saddle and carried it up with him. He had left the axe up in the brush, and what with the quicker climb and the use of the rope to make a bigger bundle, he figured he was ahead of Will after the second trip.

He was. When the mustanger said there was enough wood piled up, only half the mescals had been cut. Will pointed with his chin, Indian fashion. "You search 'em out over there. Don't take any that are dried out. The ants will have got all the sugar."

They were about eight mescals short when dark stopped them. Will squatted and made a little fire out of twigs, got a skillet and jerky from his saddle-bag, added water, and put the mess over the little fire to cook. When the water began to bubble, he sifted in cornmeal from a small cloth sack. "Not bad food," he said, noticing Dan's face. "You'll remember it when you been with the band a few weeks."

It wasn't bad, Dan found, when time came to eat it. The jerky was more heavily peppered than what the Rikers had, but it was recognizable as something to eat.

Will scoured out the skillet with a little sand and boiled more water for weak coffee. There was no sugar. "We finish up here midmorning and go to work," Will said. "Which band do you favor, Dan?"

Dan just stared at him. "I don't know. I thought we'd ride around until we saw mustangs."

Will shook his head. "There is none so blind as them who will not see. We crossed tracks of three bands and two lone studs today. Sure, winded over and double-tracked by cattle, but there to read if you know your business."

Dan said, "I'm sorry."

"What for, partner? You are here to learn. I could tell you how to read mustang sign, but better I show you right on the prairie. Even if it takes an extra day. The reason hardly anybody makes out mustanging, no matter how they go about it, is they don't know how to read. A man can tell from the hoof marks and the droppings, how big the stallion is, how healthy his mares, how many. It pays."

Dan finished his coffee—there wasn't enough coffee in the water to keep a mouse awake—and rinsed the cups. He put them down by the fire for morning and was ready to turn in.

The mustanger sighed, and said, "Let us lay down and rest. Heavy work tomorrow."

Dan lay there until he heard, from the soft breathing, that Will was asleep. Then he got up, very carefully not making any noise, and climbed a little ways up the butte.

There wasn't a drop of moisture in the air. There wasn't any moon. A million stars must have been out, and from the height to which he'd climbed, he could see all of Texas, it seemed.

He sat there, thinking about the strange life of the man who now called him partner. Except for Will, he knew no one, had heard of no one, who really understood the wild horses. He was going to learn about them, which made him a very lucky boy. He guessed there wasn't a luckier one around, even if he was going to have to live on dry jerky and roasted mescal for a long, long time.

13

Morning, and jerky stew and weak coffee, and then Will handed Dan a saddle shovel—just a D-spade with the handle cut down—and said, "Dig us a pit, partner. About two feet deep, and maybe four feet by four feet. Move out from the butte a ways, and you'll miss the rocks."

Dan missed the rocks all right, but it was a hard job anyway with a shovel that was half blade. About all that could be said of the work was that it was better than digging a hole with your bare hands or your hat brim.

But the hole got dug, while Will continued to gather mescal buds, going farther and farther afield for them. Once he came by, and said, "Start dragging up those bundles of twigs you've got, and burn them in the pit."

Grazed full, both horses had come into camp. They followed Dan as he went back to get the first bunch of twigs, but when he had dragged them to the pit and struck fire to them, the ponies threw up their tails and ran ten, twenty feet away. Then they stopped, turned, and went back to watching him. They weren't really scared, he knew, they just felt playful.

He heaped the fire high, but it burned down fast. The twigs weren't any more firewood than twisted grass would have been. Still, Will, beginning to bring the cut agave stalks up, seemed satisfied. "Burn it all down, Dan. We'll get coals enough for our use."

Finally all the wood was burned. A good foot of coals and ashes was left in the pit. Will threw the mescals in, and said, "Start shoveling dirt on them."

When they finished, Dan was a mess, from sweat and soot and dust. He looked over and saw that his dark partner was just as messy. No one riding up could have told which was the one who had started out white.

"We sure look awful," Will said. "But we'll look worse before we look better. Couple of weeks from now, our very own mamas would shoo us out of camp

if we rode up. . . . Saddle up, Dan, and ride around
the foot of the butte. There's always a spring under
one of these ridges. Fill both the water bottles, and
I'll stand guard here."

"Guard?"

"No Apaches around, but Lipans is just about
where you find them. And a mescal roast would tempt
the most honest Apach'. Stealing from outside the
tribe is a highly respected thing to do among my red
brothers."

Dan thought he was going to hear more about the
strange life that Will had led, but something had
made the mustanger dreamy and thoughtful. So Dan
threw Sherry's saddle on, tied the water bottles behind him, and rode out, following the base of the
butte.

The riding was rocky, but he kept his eyes on the
ground as did Sherry, and they went at a walk. Dan
was anxious to find the mark of wild horses, to make
up for what he'd missed yesterday, but he had no
luck. If any band had passed that way, they'd left no
sign he could read.

The first spring he came to was bubbling cold and
clear from a cleft in the rock over his head. The water
fell in a thin stream, disappearing into the sandy soil,
and it would have been easy to hold the bottles under
the waterfall.

The morning was getting along, the sun was warm,

and it would have been nice to take a shower. But what Will had said about looking worse before they looked better clanged in Dan's head, and he thought he'd better ask before he bathed. Better taste the water, too, before he filled the bottles.

He was right to be careful. The bitter, soapy taste of alkali was strong in the spring.

So he rode on and hoped he'd be able to tell Will how smart he had been. But he was pretty sure the mustanger would take it in stride, saying something like "of course," instead of "good boy," as Mr. Riker would have done. Will lived by a tougher set of standards than the maverickers around and about him.

The second spring Dan found had good enough water, but it was just a seep. He had to dig a hole in the sand and pat the sides flat for it to fill up enough to hold a canteen. It took half an hour to fill the bottles.

Will was stretched out on the ground when he got back. "Turn your pony loose," he said. "Mescals will take another hour to get good and sweet."

Dan got down, stripped off the saddle, took the blanket and flipped it upside down on the sand to dry. Will jumped to his feet and snatched up the saddle pad, wet with Sherry's sweat. "Rub this on you," he said.

Frowning, Dan did so. He rather liked the smell

of a sweaty horse, but dried on his face the sweat was sticky and itchy. He scraped at it with his fingers.

"Leave it on," Will said. "You and me, we're going to become horses, inside and out, in head and body and soul."

The mustanger spoke with such force, so seriously, that Dan couldn't think he was joking. Will was like a minister talking about his religion.

Dan said, "How do we do that?"

"You'll see, you'll see. Getting to know wild horses is the greatest thing in the world."

Golly, Dan thought, I've hooked up with a madman, for sure. And yet, nothing Will ever had done seemed crazy. Furthermore, the maverickers all had seemed to think he was the greatest mustang catcher on the prairies. So Dan kept his mouth shut and just rested.

Will didn't say anything more while they waited for the mescals to roast and, after they had dug them up, to cool. Then he looked at the sky. "Good time to start out," he said. "Won't be any rain till tomorrow at the soonest. Unwrap your bedroll, and let's stow this good food in the groundsheets."

The groundsheet of Dan's bedroll was canvas, which he and his father had paraffined three times. It would keep him dry on the wettest night. Will's was only gutta-percha, quilt-stitched to a piece of canvas tarpaulin. Dan's father had said that he didn't care for that kind of protection: "It stiffens up and cracks when it gets cold. The Army issued them to us, but the boys used to throw them away when they could get a good homemade paraffin like this one."

But one sheet bent as easily as the other. Will put fifteen mescals in each, and folded and wrapped them till there was a bulky package to tie on the two mares. "One left over, and cool enough to eat now," he said. "Let's have it."

Grinning all over, he took out his pocketknife and cut the roasted agave bud across. "Watch me." He shucked off the half-burned leaves with his knife, dug out a chunk of the heart, and put it in his mouth. Then he chewed and grinned all at the same time.

Dan took his own knife and imitated his partner. The roasted meat tasted remarkably good, slightly sweet, but a little acid, too, to keep it from becoming cloying. He chewed and swallowed with pleasure, and then was aware that he was grinning as widely as Mesteño Will was.

"You need jerky to go with it," Will said. "Or some kind of meat, and jerky is the only thing you can carry when you are a horse. Raw meat spoils, and if you tried cooking, the rest of the horse band would call you outlaw. But the mescal, that's what sticks to your ribs and keeps you feeling good. When I quit working, get too old to go mustanging, I'm going to make camp in a big patch of agave and eat nothing but mescal all through my old age."

Maybe he *was* crazy, Dan thought, but he certainly knew how to get something fine to eat in a country where a white man would starve to death. No wonder Will's Apache relatives had been so hard for the Army to put down. Everyone said you couldn't starve an Apache out, no matter what kind of country you ran him into.

When they finished eating, Dan was stickier and itchier than ever. But Will assured him that in a few days he wouldn't notice. "Too much going on. Now we have to go bury all this good food."

They saddled up, tied the canvas bundles behind them, and mounted. Will stood in the stirrups and looked all around, squinting at the distant buttes. "I know just where I am now," he said. "My camp lies over yonder." He pointed. "We'll ride us a wide circle to there, or thereabouts, and get down to business."

Once again Will rode with his eye on a fixed spot a little ahead and to the left of his horse's front hoof. Dan, who was accustomed to swiveling his eyes around for holes or cattle or anything else of interest, did the same.

"There," Will said, right after they had buried the

first two mescals about four miles apart. "There's a band. What do you make of it?" He pointed at unshod horse tracks on the prairie. "Get down, study it. I can tell from the saddle, but you have it all to learn."

Dan got out of the saddle and sat on his heels, holding Sherry's lines. "I'd say about fifteen horses," he said finally.

Will dismounted, too, but continued standing, leaning against Blue Streak's side. "Seventeen," he said. "A stallion, somewhat lame in the off-front leg, but that is just from his hoof splitting. Old, maybe ten or eleven, which is long gone for a wild one. Mostly they don't live more than seven, eight years, which is one reason I do not mind catching them up. They will be cared for, sheltered and fed, and live to a ripe old age. Might almost like that for myself, but I reckon not. All right. One stud. Ten mares, about six hundred pounds each, three of them too old to be worth much, but seven prime, good young ones. Three suckling colts, two yearling fillies, and one colt, long yearling or short two-year-old."

"How can you tell that?"

"Looky there," Will said. He seemed almost a kid, he was so happy and carefree. "The stallion keeps trying to run him off—see the tracks there, and there— which is what a stud does to a boy horse when he gets about two years old. One he horse to a band is the rule, though babies don't count. That's why I can't tell you whether the three sucklings are little boy babies or little girl babies."

As the dark hand gestured, Dan could, in truth, read a lot more than he had thought possible. The little hoof marks ran right alongside the big marks of their mothers, and what he would have thought a little while ago was one colt or four became, clearly, three. He said, "I guess you figure the weight of the mares from how deep their tracks are."

"Right," Will said.

"And what's more," Dan said, "you can tell most of them are close-coupled, from the way the back hoofs strike near the front."

"I didn't mention that. But you're right. You'll make a mustanger. Close-coupled fetches the best money. Every extra inch between the last rib and the hipbone is a point against a horse. Long back, tired back, is what they say. I'd like to know what colors they run, but we'll learn that when they go through brush and leave some hair. Cowboys and back-East farmers got some preference as to color, which is kind of silly. We're lucky to cut such a good band the first day out. Sometimes I search a week."

Dan laughed. "You can't fool me. You spotted these tracks yesterday, while I was moon gazing around the prairie."

"I spotted them a week ago," Will said. "But I

wasn't going to tell you. Didn't want to spoil the fun of being in from the first for you."

"I'm not here for fun," Dan said.

"You're a good boy," Will said. "A very good boy, and I'm sure glad we're partners."

14

They buried the last of the mescals not five miles from Will's camp, and Dan thought they would ride in and have a cooked meal. But Will said, "No. Hang around where a man has been camping, and you get to smell like a man, from smoke and salt bacon and all kinds of man things that you and I can't smell now, but will be able to when we are horses."

So they rode back toward where the horse band's tracks had cut their trail. There they unsaddled and slept in their blankets and saddle pads after eating mescal and jerky. It was a dry camp, and they had to go easy on their canteens, but Will said that didn't matter. "From now on, we'll have all the water we want, and we drank up good before we left the butte."

Morning was an easy matter: roll up the sleeping blankets, throw the saddles on the horses, and ride. No washing, no fire making, and they could chew cold mescal and jerky just as well in the saddle as sitting on the ground. Both of them rode now with their eyes on the partly blown-away tracks of the horse band.

"We'll take up with them about noon," Will said. "Or maybe after. It doesn't signify. There's no place horses can go that horses can't follow."

"Supposing they run into an outfit of mustangers?"

"Then we start off fresh after another band. But I don't think they will. There's no mustangers working around here, or we would have heard. A few years ago there were mustangers all over the prairie, but they gave up. Catching mavericks is easier, though I don't cotton to it myself."

Ride and ride, and pass up good cows that could be branded with the Prescrip iron—if they had an iron along, and if Will carried a rope, which he didn't.

They passed a butte where water draining down had made a green meadow, called a *cienega* in that country. Plainly the horse band had tarried there, cropping at the lush grass. Horse droppings were all over the place, and Dan even could see the grass springing back up where hoofs had pressed it down.

"Less than an hour's head on us," Will said. "Old Splithoof really let them take their ease here. Let's ride."

They rode. Blue Streak and Sherry went along at an easy pace. Will didn't seem in a hurry, and, as the heat of the day mounted, neither did the mares. The only sweat they put out was along the front edge of the saddle pads, and where the reins rubbed their neck. From time to time, Will wiped this lather away with the edge of his hand and smeared it on himself.

So did Dan, hesitantly, and not on his face and neck, but on his pants and shirt. He had a strong idea that his mother wouldn't approve of his new way of living, but if the subject ever came up, he could say that he'd done as his boss told him to, which was the way she had taught him. That excuse was weak, but there was a strong chance he would get to bathe and wash his clothes before they ever saw his folks again, so he stopped worrying.

Dan got a little dizzy, riding on and on under the blue bowl of the sky, not going anyplace at all, just drifting along the horse tracks. This wasn't like riding to find mavericks, or going to a place like Stein's store, or tracking down an outfit's camp. Any outfits that were out cattle branding were a long ways away, for they saw no dust clouds, and very few sky clouds either. The day was one of the clearest the prairie had ever had. As the sun got overhead and the shadows went under the horses' bellies, tracks of Splithoof and his band became fainter.

Then Blue Streak whinnied, and Will broke into a broad grin. "We are there," he said. "If you have anything to say, get it said. It may be two weeks before we talk again. Maybe longer."

Sherry was dancing a little, but Dan petted her neck and she gentled down. They came up out of a little dip in the prairie, and there was the band, spread out before them.

There was no mistaking Splithoof. His mares and colts were grazing, but he stood with his head up, watching, once in a while dipping down, snatching up a strong mouthful of grass, and chewing it with his head up again. The mares, on the other hand, chewed head down, just raising their mouth to snap at flies or look to their stud to make sure everything was all right.

There was no mistaking the two-year-old colt either. He grazed off to one side, and Dan could see that he was afraid of joining the band. There were sores on his neck where Splithoof had bitten him trying to make him go away and start his own family.

"Papa on the watch," Will said softly. "It's not always that way. Sometimes one of the mares plays watchdog. Well, we'll change all that."

Dan didn't know what he meant, but it didn't matter.

Splithoof had seen them now. He threw up his head even higher and whistled through his nostrils, the noise that only a stallion could make. At once all the mares were head up and bunching. The little suckling colts and fillies ran into their mother's side and gave up their baby play of chasing each other.

Playing tag they had called it when Dan was a colt. Then he realized what he had said to himself and grinned. Will was right. He was turning into a horse already.

Will pulled up, gathering his reins lightly, and Blue Streak stopped. Dan stopped Sherry alongside his partner, and they sat, easy in the saddle, while Splithoof stared at them. "We're out of rope range," Will whispered, "and he knows it. A smart old he horse."

They were out of rope range, but in easy eyesight. Dan was surprised to see that two of the mares—or maybe more, but he could see two—wore brands on their near flanks. He halfway remembered cowboys at Stein's and places muttering that the wild horses were a nuisance; they stole any mares a man owned. The Mexican vaqueros, Dan knew, would not ride a mare, maybe for that reason.

After a while the suckling colts fanned out again, and then a mare or two dropped her head and went back to grazing. A little later Splithoof bowed his neck and came trotting around the band, to their side. Then he stood proud and trumpeted through his nose, challenging them. But when they did nothing about getting closer, he walked off, through his band, and kept on walking. The mares and their colts followed him also at an easy walk.

The two-year-old colt followed at a safe distance, doing more whinnying than grazing. His voice hadn't changed yet, and he couldn't whistle like his father.

Sherry would have liked to join the band, but when she saw how quiet Blue Streak was, she stayed with her old friend. Will rode along, silently, not fiddling with his lines or moving in the saddle. Gradually Splithoof stopped looking at the mounted men.

An hour or two after they had sighted the band, and about the same time before sundown, the two-year-old gave up trying to join the main band and came back to follow Will and Dan and their mares. Sherry kicked out at him once, and then acted as if he'd always taken the packhorse place in their little train. Blue Streak had been through this routine before. She looked at the colt once and went on following the band, nibbling as well as the sidebars of her bit would let her.

The newcomer was a nice-looking colt, not big-headed as so many of the wild horses were. His color was a dark, bright red. In his mind, Dan named him Wattle, after the neck ornaments on some turkeys he'd once raised. The little stud's coat was just the same color.

Dan was aching to tell Will the colt's name, but he didn't dare talk till Will did. If ever. Mustanging might pay—though Dan still didn't see how a man and a boy, or two men for that matter, would ever get the wild broomtails into Will's small corral—but running down mustangs this way was the lonesomest thing in the world.

Sun was going down and twilight starting, when Will raised his hand and pointed. Off to the south-east a little ways there were rays going to the setting sun. A rider didn't have to be long on the prairie to know that they meant a water hole.

Will tapped Dan's arm and smiled, and then twisted his face into a most strange shape and whis-tled through his mouth and nose at the same time. He sounded like a stallion, but his call was not like any of the noises Splithoof had made up to now. Then Will shortened his lines and neck-reined Blue Streak around toward the water hole.

Wattle—Dan was going to call him Wattie for short—came around without being told, and Dan tapped Sherry's neck to turn, too, though he didn't really have to. When he craned his head around, he still could watch the wild mares.

Splithoof was rearing a little, his front hoofs—including the split one—going up in the air maybe two feet, and then coming down with a thud that Dan could hear clearly a hundred yards and more away. Many of the mares already had put their head up and were trotting after Will in the loose-gaited, sloppy trot of untrained, unbred stock.

Splithoof trumpeted. Some of the mares turned back to him, but more than half the band were following Will, who surely had said, "Water," in mustang language.

As the mares came up, Wattie moved so close to Dan's knee that he could have reached out and petted the young stud. But he kept his hands in and let Will lead.

Splithoof whistled and went into a run, making a circle around the men and the red colt and charging to get in front of them, but on the same line for the same water hole. About a third of the mares went around with him, and the rest just kept on the way they had been going.

Will and Dan and Wattie were now in the middle of the band, and in that way they went on to the water hole, which they reached a half an hour later.

When they were in the cattails around the water, and the first mares were already drinking, Will spoke for the first time, although in a whisper. "Let your hoss drink as she wants to. She'll have to strain the water around her bit."

Dan nodded and moved his heels a tiny bit. Sherry got the message and went forward, as she'd wanted to. But Blue Streak and Will stayed back, Will tall in the saddle and looking in all directions.

On the other side of the water hole, Splithoof stood tall, head back and eyes flashing, as he looked out, too, to make sure nothing attacked his mares and colts while they had their head down in the water.

Several of the mares went down on their knees, and then let go altogether, rolling in the cool water. Sherry would have liked to roll, too, but she was too well trained to try.

The suckling colts were racing in the shallows, splashing water like kids in a mud puddle. Wattie, still youngster enough to want to play, ran with them. But then he got too close to Splithoof. The stud lowered his head and charged him, teeth bared. The long yellow teeth clicked menacingly just above Wattie's neck, and though the colt wasn't hurt, he squealed and raced back to his friends Dan and Sherry.

Without thinking, Dan moved his mare between the young stud and the old man of the band. Splithoof, hind feet in the water, front hoofs up on the sand, pulled up, red-eyed and glaring. The red colt stayed well behind Dan.

Dan took his rein ends and flicked Splithoof's nose. At once he was afraid he had done wrong. He should have waited for Will to order him before he did anything like that. But Wattie was his friend, and he had moved to protect him before he thought.

Splithoof reared a little bit and came down on the sand. Where he landed his hoofs went deep enough to dig water and send it splashing. Then he turned and trotted through the shallows to the other side of the pond, where he had stood guard before.

When the mares left the water, they split about even. Half came out on the side where the men and Wattie were, and half went to Splithoof. Then Will and the stallion moved to take their drink, though Blue Streak did the drinking for the mustanger.

Afterward the divided band moved back from the water. But they joined up again, a ways out, and moved on as a single group.

15

Dinner that night was just jerky and water; they had eaten all of the roasted agave bud during the day. It wasn't much to stick to a boy's ribs. Half an hour after he had finished, Dan was hungry again, but the idea of chewing more of the salty, spicy dried meat didn't attract him.

Will rolled his bedding out and used his saddle for a pillow. Dan did the same thing. Blue Streak and Sherry were out grazing with the band, but one by one the mares came in and lay down, and finally the stallion did too. He picked a place that was a little bit—very little bit—higher than the rest of the bedding ground, and Dan was sure that he'd be up at once in case anything threatened his mares.

Dan lay on his side, facing Will, and tried to go to sleep. But he had not done enough work to make him tired. His brush cutting was far behind him, and the afternoon had been spent just lounging in the saddle. When something nudged him in the small of the back, he almost yelled. But he clapped his hand to his mouth and choked his fear—or what have you—down and looked over his shoulder.

Wattie, that bright red youngster, had come up to sleep with his nose against the back of his new friend.

From Will's bed came a soft chuckle. "You have made you a pal, Partner Dan."

"I thought we couldn't talk."

"I have been thinking. Like I said, horses couldn't be broken if they didn't want to be. They like men. I think maybe they will like it if we talk to each other, real soft. . . . I never had a partner before."

"Talking sounds good. I was beginning to think maybe I'd forgotten how."

Another easy chuckle. "Too hungry to sleep? Tomorrow we'll catch up with some of that good roasted mescal."

Dan felt his mouth watering. Will was right. Roasted agave was good eating, maybe not as good

as his mother's cooking, but a lot better than jerky without mescal. "How?"

"Why, Dan, have a little faith in your partner. I know where we buried the food. I'm Apache enough to smell it out, if I have to. Tomorrow I'll start curving the herd, just a little, not much, and they'll cross over one of our food caches. You'll see."

"Think I could smell out food myself about now."

Another laugh. "This is going to be easier than I thought. Splithoof is about through; he's old to be leading such a big band of mares. We got us a big aid when your little stud there took to you so strong."

"His name's Wattie, for turkey wattle."

"He is just about that color." Then Will said, "Hush a moment."

Splithoof was lumbering to his feet, fast as a horse could get up. Dan raised his own head and looked. The stallion was sniffing the air through his huge nostrils; he turned in all directions. Then he kneeled and lay down again.

"Just coyotes," Will said after a minute. "They'll go wide of a big band like ours. A lone mare with a colt might interest them, but not a lot of horses. Way I usually work, Dan, is to take over the lead of the band, little by little, and slow, slow as an old turtle. I'm smarter than any horse, any man is, and I know the country. I lead them to better water, better grass than the stud—sometimes it's an old mare—has been doing. Truth is, no horse likes to think; it's his nature to live. So the leader is glad to turn the job over to me after a while."

Dan's reaction was to be a little angry. Sherry had been his friend a lot longer than Will had, and the mustanger was calling her stupid, along with all other horses. But Will spoke the truth. Maybe the words weren't just the right ones. Still, they explained how a horse gave in to a man and became a pet and a work helper, when he was so much bigger he could kill any unarmed man. Look how Wattie had decided to join up with Dan.

Will said, "I love horses myself. But facts are facts. Now I been thinking. If Splithoof was in his prime, your little Wattie would have been run off half a year ago. Some of the mares must have been siding with him, and Splithoof knows it. . . . You ever ride bareback?"

"Sure."

Will chuckled. "Maybe this time you're going to be senior partner. Maybe you're the one who's going to lead us to home and money, 'stead of me. Tomorrow I'd like to see you on foot. If your Sherry mare won't follow you, I can lead her by her lines."

"She'll follow me."

"Don't get huffy. Some horses never do learn to

follow without being led. . . . You take every chance
you can to pet that Wattie horse. Get your hands all
over him, so he gets used to you. Then, late tomorrow,
maybe the next day, try sliding belly down onto his
back. Handle his head good, Dan. You'll want to put
a rope hackamore on him."

Dan said, "Golly!"

"I'm giving you my half interest in that colt," Will
said. "What mares and colts we get, we split down the
middle like real partners. But the colt is yours. A man
doesn't want to sell the very first mustang he ever
takes, and you have taken that one just fine."

"You sure?"

Will said, "If you were to saddle up Sherry and ride
out right now, he would be riding at your tail like an
old Army packhorse. Believe me."

"He's mighty handsome."

"You're getting him young enough so he won't
grow up looking mustangy. He'll shape into a dandy
horse. First year or so, of course, you can only ride
him a little, or you'll make him swaybacked. A grown
man couldn't ride him at all for a year. Lucky you're
light."

"I'll be lighter if we don't get to some food tomorrow."

"Go to sleep, Dan. Tighten your belt."

Dan muttered good-night and closed his eyes. Then

he rolled over, so his back was to Will. Softly he put a hand out and rested it on Wattie's hard cheekbone. The colt fluttered his lips a little, like a horse whinnying a greeting, opened his eyes, and closed them again.

It won't be day after tomorrow that I lie on his back, Dan thought. It'll be tomorrow itself, and maybe not even in the afternoon.

And then, just as he was falling asleep, he realized that he was a full-share partner with Will, not just called "partner" in the Texas custom. The agreement didn't seem right, but Mesteño Will was hard to argue with. Still. . . .

16

Wattie was a good, quiet sleeper, which was a blessing. Though not yet full grown, he was larger than a lot of the broomtail mares, and if he'd thrashed around, Dan could have gotten a kick that would not have waked him up laughing.

Sometime during the night Dan was awakened, but not by Wattie. He opened his eyes. The moon had come up, and one by one the wild mares were getting up to graze. By raising his head a little, he could see Splithoof standing on guard at the far edge of the bedding grounds. Blue Streak and Sherry got up and moved after the wild mares. Trained to come on call, they were used to grazing free at night.

Finally Wattie got up too, his lips whickering a little. Instead of going off to fill his belly, however, he just stood.

Dan rolled over to face Will as he heard the mustanger laughing. Not whispering now, Will said, "You have yourself a problem, partner. That little stud is going to starve if you don't go with him while he eats. I won't say I haven't seen it before. I guess there is hardly anything a horse can do I have not seen, but it's a rare thing. Don't worry. Daytime he'll move out on the grass clumps as long as he can keep you in sight."

Dan was already pulling his boots on. "Will the mares come back if you stay here?"

"They could and they could not. No telling in full moon. But it's a sure thing they'll water at the same hole we passed, that being the closest, so we'll move our beds nearer there. Any panthers or bears that come down—and they are rare on the prairies—won't go near a human."

He whistled softly for Blue Streak, and said, "I hope old Splithoof doesn't take that for a stallion challenge. I'm not of a mind to fight a wild stud without a full night's sleep."

Blue Streak came in at once, with Sherry only a

little behind her. The mustangers saddled and bridled, rolled their bedding and strapped it up without talking.

When they rode out, Wattie followed them, which didn't surprise Dan.

Will pulled up after about a half an hour, nearer the water hole, though still in fair grass. He got down, stripped the gotch-eared bridle off Blue Streak, pulled the knot out of the cinch strap, and was rolling out his bed again before Dan's foot was on the ground. And before Dan had put his own bed alongside and walked out after Sherry to get Wattie on good grass, Will was, to all appearances, sound asleep.

Five minutes later Dan was too, blanketless and with his arms locked around his knees as he sat on the prairie. The last thing he heard was the noise of Wattie's teeth pulling up the clumped grass.

Sunrise woke him, and he stood up. Wattie and Sherry and Blue Streak were all down, sleeping again, the colt nearest to him. Dan stretched, feeling his shoulders uncreak. Then he bent and rubbed his knees. The prairie shone silver with dew; it had been a wetter night than usual.

Blue Streak got up when she heard him moving and started off, walking slowly toward where she had left Will. Sherry looked at Dan, and then started trailing the other mare.

Dan called Sherry's name, and she came back to him. He shinnied up on her back, not even bothering to take his belt off and put it around her neck to guide her. She would answer to his knees fairly well if he had to turn her, but he counted on her following Blue Streak. Wattie came alongside Dan's right knee.

It was a slow walk back to where Will was bedded down, with the horses stopping to eat here and there. But Sherry's body under him and the sun on his head and back and shoulders all felt good after sleeping sitting up through the dewy night.

Dan leaned over and rested his right hand on Wattie's back as they went, just behind the withers. The young stud didn't even look around, and they went on that way for a little while. Then Dan couldn't stand to wait any longer. He figured he was still out of sight of Will, who might get mad if he saw Dan breaking his orders to handle Wattie all over for a while before he tried putting weight on his back.

Dan swung both legs over to Sherry's offside and rode that way for a minute. Finally he put his right leg out and shoved himself over and landed square on Wattie's back.

The colt reared with surprise. His head came around for Dan's left knee, teeth bared. But the teeth snapped together a good four inches forward of that knee, and the rear never developed into anything much at all. Quickly Wattie settled down, walking clumsily because he wasn't used to carrying anything but himself, but walking proud nevertheless.

They came into camp. Will had the blankets rolled and was strapping the second roll to its saddle. He let the job go and stood up straight, his hands on his hips, squinting in the rising sun, studying the group coming toward him.

Then he dropped his hands, and said, "You Blue Streak, come here."

Dan slid down and kneeled to finish tying his bedroll to his saddle. But as he bridled and saddled his mare he wished he was dressing Wattie for the day's riding.

As though he could read Dan's mind, Will said, "Now, listen, partner. I don't want to catch you riding that good colt more than five minutes at a time, three times a day, for a year. I've never ruined a young horse's back yet, and I don't want to partner with anyone who does."

Dan said, "Yes, sir." Now seemed the right time to call Will "sir" whether he approved or not.

They beat the wild band to the water hole, which was a blessing, for the three horses in their string drank quietly without muddying it, and Dan could fill his canteen and Will's with nice, clean water.

When they heard Splithoof's family coming in,

Will picked up his lines and they moved back from the cattails and arrowweed to dry ground to let the wild ones water. "He'll fight your Wattie now," Will said, staring at Splithoof from under the tattered brim of his hat. "I've seen it happen a hundred times."

"What's that?"

"A band of broomtails splits when a colt comes up to stud age. If we're lucky, most of the mares will go with us, but a few will stick with the old man. That is, until a full-grown young stud comes along and really fights old Splithoof."

"Will he get killed?"

"Not all at once," Will said. His voice was sad. "He'll be driven off and nearly die of lonesomeness. Then he'll seek out another band, try and fight its stud, and get beaten again. The second time, or maybe the third, he'll get hurt so bad his wounds will kill him off."

"Golly. Can't we—"

The mustanger said in a low voice, "You know we can't. It's a hard life the wild ones lead. That's why I never mind catching them and selling them to someone who'll look after them. It just about doubles, maybe triples, their lives. But who'd want Splithoof? You'd never break a stallion that's run loose that long, and if you did, who'd want him, ruined hoof and all?"

This bleak future made Dan feel awful, though he had no great love for Splithoof. But the mares were coming up from the water and gathering around them, as if they had known the mustangers and their mares all their lives. Staying sad was hard when they were being accepted by the wild bunch.

Will muttered to Dan to stay back with Wattie and Sherry as they moved out on the long day's traveling. "Keep the colt away from Splithoof. I'm going up and curve the course, or we'll be eating jerky again today."

As the mares and their colts started moving they thinned out so everybody could get grass. Dan saw Will from time to time. The dark mustanger was in the middle of the band at noon, riding slumped in the saddle, lines loose and long in his hand. But two hours into the afternoon, he was up toward the front of the band, riding alongside Splithoof and a few feet off to one side. When he turned Blue Streak with quiet flippings of his reins, the band came after him.

Dan had no watch, but he figured it was about four when he saw Will slip out of the saddle and kneel on the ground, digging with his machete blade. Back in the saddle, Will held up a roasted mescal, and Dan felt himself grinning like a fool.

They ate roasted agave bud that night, and the next night, and the next. Every day was the same, with Dan staying in the drag of the horse herd, back where Wattie wouldn't get into a fight with Splithoof.

The work was dull and incredibly dirty. When they

watered at night, Dan would scrub at his face and hands with sand and water, but Will said that they couldn't use soap, even if they had brought it. The smell was too manlike for the broomtails to accept.

At night Dan and Will could talk a little, but by the third night, there wasn't much to talk about. Each day Will was taking more and more charge of the band. From his place back in the dust, Dan could see that Will was leading now, and that Splithoof was even trusting the dark man to keep a lookout while the stallion grazed.

One by one the mares were taking on personalities to Dan, and he could see why Will claimed that he turned into a horse when he was mustanging. There was Starhead and her colt Bigfoot, and old Granny Graynose, and so on. Dan could imagine that if the trail went on for weeks—as Will said some of his had— he would be gossiping at night about how Longtooth had edged Scarneck away from a juicy-looking bunch of grass, or how Whitebelly thought her filly, Knobknees, was too good to play with Crossback's Blaze.

Then, once in a while, a breeze brought an odor, or an old tune ran through Dan's head, and he would be full of longing for some of his mother's pancakes and sorghum, or for the days when he had ridden with his father, talking about everything under the sun and roping mavericks, or for going to Stein's store and chatting about people and things past and things to come. He wasn't a horse, and he guessed he really didn't want to be one. But becoming just another member of the band was quite a temptation.

The one thing he looked forward to—except for watering at night and scrubbing off a little of the accumulated dirt—was slipping over on Wattie's back three or four times a day and riding the colt for a few minutes. There was power in the young body that there never had been in any horse Dan had straddled before, and he answered to Dan's knees as if he were reading his rider's mind; maybe he was.

One thing he wasn't was hungry. The more Will led the herd, the more mescals they caught up with, and Dan could have chewed all day long if he'd needed to. Roasted mescal was good food; it tasted all right and it stuck to his ribs. The outer layer held all the sand in which it had been roasted and reburied, and when Dan stripped that off, he had nice clean food, sticky, but clean and gritless.

Still—

On the fifth night, Will asked him, "How do you like mustanging?"

"Fine, Will, fine."

"Really, partner? I kind of doubt it. It's all right for me, but I got me a bellyful of mankind."

Dan didn't say anything. He had known all along

that there was a story behind the dark mustanger, but asking a man about his past was neither Texan nor polite.

"Came the War, in '61," Will said slowly, "and word got to me. I figgered I better do somethin' about it, slavery having driven my father west, and me being part black. So I headed east."

Will shook his head sadly. Dan was half holding his breath. He might be the very first person in all the world to hear the whole story of Mesteño Will.

"Sure wasn't like I'd thought it would be, like the Day of Jubilee my papa used to sing of. Wasn't no black regiments where I come up with the War, and only use a white regiment had for colored was to be servant to the officers. Dust boots and polish spurs. No kinda life at all for a man who'd ridden free on the prairies. . . ."

Dan thought. His father had said there had been colored regiments in the Union Army, and that they'd fought well.

Without Dan asking anything, Will answered his question. "Finally cotched up with a regiment whose faces were black as mine, except for the officers. Hid out two, three days watching, and then I knowed I was too Apache to join up at all. All that drillin' and about-facin' and white officers yellin' orders, while the colored took them. So I headed back west to my lonely life. I don't know what I am. Not Apache, not Negro, and sure enough not white. . . ."

"You're a mustanger," Dan said. "Half horse. I'm getting that way myself."

Will chuckled softly. "All right, partner," he said. Then his voice got as brisk as it dared, there on the bedding grounds. "We're going to make our play tomorrow," Will said. "I've never gotten this far in so little time, but I'm going to take a chance. Dan, I have to ask you. Cut me about seven feet off your throw rope, will you?"

Dan was startled. Cutting a lariat was something a mavericker just didn't do. But he was a mustanger, not a mavericker now. So he said, "Sure," took his clasp knife out, and opened it. The rope was tied to the saddle against which he lounged. Still he waited, hoping Will had been testing him.

Will said nothing, and Dan measured off a length somewhat longer than a tall man. Then he cut.

"Right," Will said. He took the rope and started knotting the end. "You do the same with your rope."

Dan nodded and watched Will's fingers, followed their movements. All around them the mares were bedding down as twilight ended. They'd come to the time of the month when the moon didn't rise till almost dawn, and night grazing had ended. As a result, they didn't make many miles during the day, but the horses weren't going anyplace anyway.

"Tomorrow," Will said, "I'll be riding in the lead, like always. But toward noon I'm going to bring my right arm straight above my head, and when I do, you and Wattie come up to me—and we'll fight Splithoof for his band. You ready?"

"Yes, sir."

"Wattie may get marked up. You may get hurt, he may get hurt, I may get hurt. But when the studs go at each other you and me will be on Wattie's side, swinging these knotted ropes, and we'll make up for how much bigger and smarter Splithoof is than Wattie. Make up, and if we are lucky make it come out our way. Are you game, Dan?"

Dan swallowed, and then said, "Yes. Wattie and I are ready." But he really didn't feel that way.

17

Next morning, as the band moved off the bedding grounds, and to last night's water hole, watching Will and Splithoof was so interesting that Dan forgot his fears for Wattie, his smaller fears for himself.

Will took the horse herd in a wide circle before he let them water. Splithoof tried to go straight to the water hole, but every time he did Will, riding Blue Streak and sitting easy in the saddle, gave a stallion's wild whistle of alarm and headed off. After a moment Splithoof followed him, and the mares followed the two leaders, old and new.

Dan could have sworn that the stallion's face looked puzzled, though he never had believed a horse could show that expression. Wattie trotted alongside Sherry, good as he always was, completely Dan's horse. His trust made Dan feel so good he wondered how Will felt with a whole band of mares and colts in his train.

When they moved out through the waterweeds, Will rode off and Splithoof trailed him, a king dethroned, a losing politician the morning after the election. But there was still some fight in the stud. His nostrils showed red, and he cropped his grass fast, then kept his head up, eyeing Will.

Sighting on the buttes, Dan saw that they were in the final stretch of the roaming. Will was aiming, in a loose circle, for his home camp and his corral. Dan never took his eyes off his dark partner, even while he was taking short, practice rides on Wattie's bare back.

Noon brought them to a butte with a spring at its foot. Will stood guard while the mares, and then Splithoof, drank. Finally Dan came up, as the stallion went back with Will to the head of the band.

Dan refilled his water bottle and let Sherry and Wattie drink a little before he led them out again after the band, his own face and hands still wet from the scrubbing in pure spring water he had given them. A horse that is going to have to run or fight is in better shape if he hasn't filled all the way up with water.

Halfway between that last butte and the mustanger camp, Dan saw Will's arm go up. The time had come.

He got down and tightened Sherry's cinch, re-mounted, and coiled the knotted rope end on his knee, with plenty of slack in the loop he held in his hand to swing with. Then his knees urged Sherry forward, through the ambling, sun-sleepy mares, past the colts that were not playing now that noon heat was on them, but just walking by their mother's side, like little kids on their way to church in Tennessee. Finally only the oldest, babyless mares were between him and the lead. Wattie was bouncing a little along-side him, sniffing the air, nostrils wide and turning red, too.

Splithoof spotted the young stud then and turned, rearing and pawing at the air, breath roaring out of his throat in a way that surely, a few weeks before, would have sent Wattie running. But the young stal-lion was ready to make his play for the job of leader. He reared, too, and even took a few steps toward Splithoof on his hind legs before coming down to make the earth tremble with a force Dan didn't know his little horse had.

The mares scattered, went off a ways and kept their heads up, much more interested in the fight than they were in food. The stallions came together, teeth bared, breath whistling, front legs striking without any great damage. Then Splithoof, the taller of the two, crooked his neck and tried to sink his long, yellow teeth into Wattie's neck.

Dan swung with his knotted clout and caught Splithoof across the mouth. Will rode in from the rear and sent his own short rope whistling across Splithoof's rump, just below the tail. The stallion hung in the air a moment, head half turned to see who had come up from behind. Then he let out another whistling roar and plunged his front hoofs to the earth, kicking out behind as strong as he could. But Will and Blue Streak were no longer there.

The minute Splithoof's attention was off him, Wattie came up and tried for a neck bite, too. But he missed, his teeth clicking, and Splithoof got him in the chest with a side kick, like a cow's. Furiously the two stallions began fighting all out, front hoofs striking each other's chests and withers, teeth clicking, so entangled that Dan couldn't get his rope in for a moment.

But Will appeared from nowhere, standing in the stirrups on Blue Streak's short back, whirling his knout around his head and bringing it down between Splithoof's ears. The old leader went down on his side, off balance. Wattie reared and tried to bring his front hoofs down on the old stud's neck, but Splithoof rolled out of the way, came up with his back to

Wattie, kicked out with his hind feet, and caught the red colt square in the chest.

Will brought his rope knot down with full strength across the big stallion's rump and spoiled a lot of the force in the kick. Dan was up front flailing away at Splithoof's head.

The stallion changed positions faster than seemed possible and struck again, not at Wattie, but at Dan and his rope. Then Dan and Sherry were half flying as Wattie hit Sherry in the shoulder to get her out of the way. Rearing like Splithoof, he was determined to fight his own fight, win his own way with the band.

The coil of rope was still in Dan's hand, with its catching loop held in his palm. An experienced cow-catcher, he could have reversed the rope and looped Splithoof's front legs, taken the turns around his saddle horn, and finished the fight right then. However, Splithoof would end up with a broken leg and maybe two. Somehow he couldn't do it. Dan was on Wattie's side, of course. Still, Splithoof was alive, and a broken leg would mean death.

A minute later Dan was glad as he ever had been in his life. Splithoof turned and trotted off, his head only half high, every bit of his hard, shining body saying he had given up. A hundred safe feet away he stopped and whistled.

Four mares, one of them with a filly at her side, heeded the call and went moving out after the stud that had led them for so long. But the rest of the band stayed back, looking to Wattie for their next move. And Wattie looked at Dan.

Will came up on Blue Streak and pointed with his chin. "Yonder lies the camp," he said, "and you lead out, partner."

Twice that afternoon they rode over places where both Dan and Will knew there were mescals buried. But neither mustanger got down to dig them up. They were on their way into camp, where there was cornmeal and bacon, part of a ham and coffee. In fact, Will, not Dan, was the one who said, "I sure wonder what people see in that roasted mescal. Maybe it's all right for a full-blooded Apache, but my father's stock in me is calling out for something else."

Dan laughed.

An hour before sundown he and Will rode into the corral, and Will started riding the edge, going all the way around the stockade to get back by the gate, while Dan, Wattie still at his side, rode as deep in as he could, and then just waited. Some of the mares shied and snorted as they came through the wide gateway, but they came. Wattie was now their leader. Finally Will closed the gate and climbed it to wave to Dan. Their band was caught, their work done.

Dan eased out of the saddle, pulled off Sherry's saddle and bridle, and threw them up on the top rail. He slipped through the rails and was free himself. Wattie whickered after him.

Dan came around, walking. Blue Streak was off a ways, grazing. "You have to leave Sherry in there awhile," Will said. "We don't dare open the gate. . . . So, come on, nursemaid."

"Huh?"

"You got you half a captive band of horses to feed and water, mustanger. You expect me to do all the work around here?"

Dan thought a moment. "I'll haul all the water and fork all the hay they can drink and eat," he said. "But not until I take me a swim and a scrub in that water hole." He sniffed. "That half of me that ain't horse is tired of smelling the half that is."

18

If Dan had thought that a mustanger's work was over when he closed the corral on a wild bunch, he learned differently. There might have been horse catchers who stopped there, but Mesteño Will was not one of them.

True, he gave his partner two days off to go home and visit his parents, and he advanced him money to take to them. Dan found his father mending well enough; Mr. Riker could walk with a cane, and he even rode a bit, now that the gentle, well-trained Sherry was back.

Dan told him, "Will says we'll put the mares and colts up for sale in about three weeks, and we hope you'll be able to get over then."

His father said, "The mares, eh? You're not selling Wattie there?" The young stud was, as always, not more than fifty feet from Dan, and from time to time he interrupted his hay eating to make sure his master was still there.

"What do you think?" Dan asked.

"I think if you did put him up for sale, I'd worry about having a crazy son."

Dan laughed. He found he could talk to his father just as he had before the accident, when they had mavericked together. But his mother had changed. She no longer reminded him to wash before eating or to go to bed early.

When Dan got back to Will's camp, he found a half dozen mares tied to the corral posts, on the outside. Each wore a hand-tied halter and had a blanket or croker sack tied on her back.

"I can slip up on them already," Will said. "We'll have, I figure, about five mares to sell as green brokes, about three to ship back east for breeders, two with a colt at their side, and the one with the filly I'm think-of keeping. You can help in the green breaking."

Dan flipped a finger at Wattie. "I brought back two sacks of oats from Stein's for Wattie."

"Good idea," Will said. "He'll grow some more on grain. But you're going to have to break him of following you the way he does or give up mustanging. You can't join up with a wild band if you have a stud along."

Dan didn't say anything.

"Going back to mavericking with your dad?" Will asked.

"I just haven't thought about it," Dan said.

Will said, "Take your time. Maybe Wattie'll settle down and stay home if you build him a good corral and give him some mares to keep him company. Maybe he'll take to your mother and want to stay home with her. And maybe you'll never go mustanging again. There's a whole life to think it over in."

That was the last ever said on the subject. The two of them worked and worked, and one by one the selected mares came under the saddle, some bucking, some rearing, and one or two really fighting.

Will didn't believe in fighting back. When a mare really objected to being ridden, he just tied her tight, handled her more, and talked to her, and she came out gentle. He was maybe the best horseman in the world, Dan thought.

The Saturday before the sale, Will sent Dan out in a wide loop that didn't get him back till sundown Sunday. He had left word at Stein's and the two other stores in that widespread prairie that Mesteño Will had horses for sale.

The sale was on a Friday. The partners got up early and rubbed the mares down until they shone. Then they changed their own clothes, ate breakfast, and waited. They didn't have long to wait. The first maverickers got there before Dan and Will had time for a second cup of coffee.

"Sure curious," Will said, watching riders, each little group under its own dust cloud, approach. "You can ride this lonesome land till your eyeballs ache for the sight of a human face and not see any soul. Then a something like this brings them all together, and, man, there is a total of them."

Dan's parents got there while the first dozen riders were looking over the mares, each cowboy's and foreman's face as still as a stone mask. No man at a horse sale anywhere ever admitted to his own best friend which horse he was interested in.

Dan could take time to unharness his family's mules, turn them out, and help his dad down from the wagon. Mr. Riker turned back, got his cane, and went striding off to the corral pretty fast. Dan put a hand up to his mother, but she hopped over the wheel without help.

"Look at my husband," she said. "I swear, he'd rather go to a horse auction than eat fresh eggs."

"I reckon most men would," Dan said. He was certainly excited himself, and he was surely not about to buy a mare.

"You ought to know," his mother said.

But Dan wasn't listening. Pasan and a half dozen riders were coming into camp. Pasan was riding the buckskin he had bought from Will; apparently man and horse had stopped going around and around.

Dan said to his mother, "There's the man who was going to brand ℞ connected when we left the country."

"He's got a good chance to see that Rikers are still here. . . . You've got things to do, Son. Don't worry about me."

By now there were a good half hundred maverickers and horse drovers there. Dan's job was to catch up the mares one at a time while Will asked for bids.

The sale went fast. Will kept referring to the mares as "the little lady my partner's now showing you," or "my partner there and I call this one Crossback," and Dan could feel the maverickers' eyes on him. They couldn't tell he was blushing, because he was red in the face from the work of leading each mare fast enough to show off her paces.

The prices were high for green-broke horses. After a while men stopped bidding under fifty, and twice the call went to a hundred.

Pasan didn't bid. He stood there, his face ugly,

scowling as mare after mare went by. Dan knew, of course, that the foreman had bought horses from Will before, and all the mavericking outfits could use extra ponies. So Pasan must have been angry because Will had partnered up with a white boy.

One of the men took advantage of a break while Dan caught a fresh mare to say, "When are you putting up the red stud colt, Will?"

"Not for sale," Will said. "He's my partner's personal project."

Pasan shot a sudden look at Dan, then looked at Wattie, then at Dan again. His thick lips formed into a silent whistle. When the bidding got to seventy-five dollars on the next mare, a golden buckskin, Pasan suddenly shouted, "A hundred and let's stop this foolin' around." He finally got Goldneck for a hundred and thirty, the highest price so far.

Then, at last, the sale was over, the men hunkering down to drink coffee from Will's pot, the riders now talking to each other, looking over what their friends had bought. Pasan had three mares in all. He knelt and felt their legs; he ran his hands all over them. Then he stood up, and his bull voice drowned out the chattering, soft-spoken cowboy voices all over the camp. "Did me a good piece of business," he boomed. "Always have got good ponies from this here Injun." The chattering hushed. "You never told me, Mesteño, what tribe your folks come from?"

Will, now sitting on the edge of the Riker wagon bed, didn't smile. He said, "Apache, Mr. Pasan. Lipan Apache."

"What I thought," Pasan said. He walked over to Dan's parents. "You Riker, I filed on Railroad Connected, figuring to blot your brand all legal when you left the county. Didn't know then you was part Injun, but I shoulda from your young'un's face. Injuns heal real fast. What are you, part Cherokee?"

"Sure," Mr. Riker said. Dan had never heard of this fact before.

"Gimme two bits, and I'll make over RR connected to you," Pasan said. "Never knew a Cherokee to quit yet. My grandmaw was half Cherokee her very own self."

Mr. Riker gravely handed over a twenty-five-cent piece. Pasan scribbled on a page of his tally book and handed the page over.

Will jumped down from the wagon and strolled over to Dan. "Stubborn old bull, isn't he? Well, welcome to the tribe, cousin. We're the same color now."

Dan had trouble not laughing out loud.

ABOUT THE AUTHOR

Richard Wormser was born in New York City and attended school there, later going to Peddie School, in Hightstown, New Jersey, and Princeton University. Returning to New York from Princeton, he worked as a newspaper reporter, in public relations, and in publishing, which led to fiction writing. In that field he quickly proved successful; his short stories appeared in rapid succession in many magazines, including *The Saturday Evening Post* and *Colliers*.

In 1937 Mr. Wormser moved to the West where he began writing novels and screen plays in addition to magazine stories. His book, *Ride a Northbound Horse*, published by Morrow, won a Spur Award from the Western Writers of America in the Best Juvenile Book category. He also has been Editor of Anthropological Publications at the Museum of New Mexico and Director of the Southwest Association on Indian Affairs.

He and his wife, who is a writer, too, now live in Santa Fe, taking frequent trips throughout the Southwest and Old Mexico.